Death Drea

J. R. Park lives in Bristol. He is the highly regarded author of *Terror Byte*, *Punch*, *Upon Waking* and *The Exchange*. He teamed up with extreme horror author Matt Shaw to co-write the satirical and brutal *Postal* in 2017, and released his fresh take on the werewolf sub-genre with *Mad Dog*. His mind has been described by one reviewer as 'the darkest place in the universe', whilst another has proclaimed him to be 'a much needed shot in the arm for gritty pulp horror.'

DEATH DREAMS
AT
CHRISTMAS

J R PARK

Death Dreams At Christmas

First Published in 2017

Copyright © 2017 J. R. Park

Artwork by Jorge Wiles.
Facebook.com/JWilesIllustrator
Twitter: @j_illustrator

Merry Christmas, you small print readers.

ISBN: 978-1-9997418-8-4

JRPark.co.uk
SinsiterHorrorCompany.com

ACKNOWLEDGEMENTS

Thank you to my superb editor, Stuart Park for his valuable feedback. His comments are a vital stage in creating my finished work, offering me alternative wording when things get clunky and picking up on details I may have missed.

Also a sincere thank you to Steph Clitheroe, Daniel Marc Chant, Sarah Taylor and Amy Ford for reading and providing feedback on early drafts of these stories. Not only did you help me polish these stories but all of you have provided inspiration for them in some shape or form.

Lastly, a huge thank you to Jorge Wiles for using his fantastic talent to take my rough sketch of the cover and turn it into something absolutely wonderful.

For Bruce and Glenda (or as I know them: Dad and Mum). You have given me so many happy Christmases and much, much more.

Contents

Please accept this horror tribute to the Christmas season as it was intended, a little piece of macabre merriment; selections of festive fear and gory entertainment to be best enjoyed in December.

Pour a glass of your favourite drink and let's get cosy.

Merry Christmas.

J. R. Park

Once A Year

Brenda:	It's almost time.
Susan:	I know.
Brenda:	He's coming, isn't he?
Susan:	You know he is. He always does.
Brenda:	At least it's only once a year.
Susan:	Count the blessings. Can you imagine if it was more? We'd have to tell the children the truth, you know?
Brenda:	Beggar's belief. The poor little blighters.
Susan:	We'd have no choice. One night is bad enough. There's no way we'd be able to protect them for any longer.
Brenda:	And we've tried everything.
Susan:	Oh haven't we just? Confusing him with all those flashing lights; in our homes, shop windows and all over the streets.
Brenda:	I swear they put more up every year.
Susan:	We've dressed up imposters to look like him. Placed statues in every garden and street corner to scare him off. But still he comes.
Brenda:	Don't forget the mince pies.
Susan:	Exactly, Brenda. Even when he does get through all those deterrents and come down from the sky, they tell us to leave out poisoned pies.
Brenda:	And the brandy.
Susan:	*(Sigh)* I wish the arsenic would actually kill the

bastard, not just make him ill.

Brenda: It's a bugger to get the stains out the carpet, isn't it?

Susan: And still he comes. Still he finds his way through all the traps, distractions and poison.

Brenda: All those blinding lights too.

Susan: Still he skulks across our roofs and crawls down our chimneys, trying to find a way in.

Brenda: Trying to find a way to our children.

Susan: Our babies!

Brenda: What kind of monster eats children?

Susan: *He* does. Gorging on the poor little souls for one night then back to his hiding place.

Brenda: One day they'll find where he goes.

Susan: I hope so, Brenda, I really do. But all these years and nothing.

Brenda: You think it's true what they say? That he's from another dimension?

Susan: Who knows? It sounds like a load of old hogwash to me, but quite frankly any explanation is as good as the next. We'll leave that to the experts. Our job is protecting our children.

Brenda: The little darlings, they're so good.

Susan: Oh yes, they are so good.

Brenda: And they're quite rightly rewarded with presents.

Susan: They stay asleep and keep right out of the way whilst we defend our homes. Look at that blade, Brenda. I spent most of the autumn sharpening that little beauty.

Brenda: Looks lethal.

Susan: I should hope so. Remember when the old chimney creeper had Alice from over the road?

Brenda: Poor Alice.

Susan: Last year my axe wouldn't have cut butter, let

alone *his* thick, scaly hide! I tried to help save her and lost an eye! He tore it right out with one of those hooked claws of his.

Brenda: You were so good to help.

Susan: It's the wonder of Christmas, Brenda. It brings people together.

Brenda: It truly does.

Susan: How many arrows have you got for your crossbow?

Brenda: Twelve.

Susan: That doesn't seem enough.

Brenda: Oh, don't worry, I have this for close quarters.

Susan: Woah! Careful where you put that, or you'll take out my other eye.

Brenda: Sorry, Susan.

Susan: Nice weapon though. I'm a little envious. Are you ready? I can hear something.

Brenda: The sound of hooves through the air.

Susan: So help me God, if I can get a piece of that bastard Rudolph I'll be made for life.

Brenda: He scares me.

Susan: And rightly so. He's got a face fit for hell itself. All those glowing red eyes and laser beam stares.

Brenda: The others are just as bad.

Susan: The way I see it, anything with tentacles growing out of their head and a face full of teeth doesn't deserve to live. Nightmares made real.

Brenda: The bells are ringing out.

Susan: Someone must have spotted him. Be on your guard.

Brenda: I'm exhausted already.

Susan: Me too.

Brenda: At least it's only once a year.

Susan: Count the blessings.

Brenda: He's coming.
Susan: I know.

The Girl With The Reindeer Tattoo

'It's not a reindeer.'

The sound of Wham's *Last Christmas* blasted from the shop speakers, its nauseatingly familiar melodies muffling the sharper edges of her annoyed tone.

Guy felt his cheeks burn with embarrassment as he watched the girl scan his purchases on the till; Christmas presents for the family. She totalled up the price, placing the CDs in a carrier bag.

Trying to regain focus on the transaction at hand he was unable to fully take his eyes off the tattoo that decorated her upper arm, running from her elbow into the sleeve of her t-shirt.

From her frosty reaction he'd clearly misidentified its design but now wasn't the time to stare and make a reassessment.

The pattern of blues, pinks and reds on her skin danced in the corner of his vision, demanding his attention, but Guy kept his concentration on the CDs, avoiding further wrath about his failed chat-up line.

'They're not for me,' he spoke with caution this time as he changed the subject.

'I figured,' she half smiled, 'you don't look like the

Chris de Burgh type.'

Guy lightly chuckled, resisting to comment on the scarlet coloured hair that hung down just past her shoulders, despite the lyrics to *Lady In Red* drifting through his mind.

'That's my Aunt's terrible taste,' he said. 'I can't stand the man, myself.'

'Good, otherwise I would definitely have no choice,' she remarked.

'No choice about what?' he asked.

'If you were buying this piece of crap for yourself then I'd definitely have to kill you,' her painted lips widened across her face, highlighting a warm grin.

Guy reciprocated and felt himself blush for the second time in as many minutes; although this time it was for an entirely different reason.

She was funny.

And flirting.

He handed her a twenty pound note and nervously fumbled with the resulting change as he tried to think of something else to say; to follow up on her good cheer. But his mouth was dry, his lips stoic against a washed up wit that deserted him at this most crucial moment.

The longer the silence grew the more impenetrable it became. His hands shook, taking all his concentration just to funnel the money into his wallet.

The tattoo on her arm caught his gaze once more, drawing his vision across her breasts as they strained at the cotton of her fitted t-shirt. Their sight sent an electric bolt of lust through his body, and although he was desperate not to make himself look foolish, his heart sank when the shock sent two pound coins slipping past his fingers and bouncing onto the lino flooring below. As they landed, they splashed in the slush from the melted snow, brought indoors by the boots of last minute shoppers this Christmas Eve.

'Shit,' he quietly muttered as he watched the golden glint of his escaped money roll under the counter.

Not saying another word, or looking back up to face the cashier, he turned and hurriedly left the shop, trying to avoid eyes of pity and ridicule as the opening chimes to Mariah Carey's festive favourite played over the queue of impatient Christmas shoppers.

*   *   *

The beer had warmed his insides and although it hadn't quite erased the anguish that haunted him since his embarrassment at the music shop this morning, it had certainly dulled the sting.

Doom laden guitar riffs squealed their distorted cries from the Jukebox of the Hobgoblin pub, providing a welcome antidote for Guy's ears; a refreshing escape from the seasonal banality of sleigh bells and kid's choirs.

He looked at his phone and wondered if he'd be seeing Christmas in alone this year. It was tradition for him and Craig, his best friend since school, to nurse a few pints until midnight, and herald the turning of the twenty-fifth with a toast and a sing-song before stumbling back home.

The wind outside rattled the windows in their frames and threw snow in all directions. Phone signals were weak and the bus service had given up an hour ago as

9

conditions on the roads became treacherous.

Craig was normally here by now.

Maybe this year the weather had beaten him.

A resentful sigh escaped Guy's lips as, with sad resignation, he looked at his empty pint glass and thought about drawing this terrible Christmas Eve to a close.

Gently, a hand touched his shoulder.

'You left these at my shop,' came the soft sounds of the cashier as she placed two pound coins on the table in front of him. 'I'm Dawn,' she said sitting on the empty stool opposite.

'G-G-Guy,' came his shocked and laboured response as he felt himself go red again; her presence bringing back his embarrassment.

'Pleased to meet you, Guy,' the smile that had disarmed him before appeared once more. 'You were shy this morning. You did that already.' Her banter was biting but playful.

He'd always liked girls with an acidic quality; caustic yet warm.

'Why don't you buy me a drink and you can find your voice whilst you're at the bar,' she winked as she spoke to soften her words.

'S-S-Sure,' Guy cursed himself for stuttering again, but headed to the bar with a growing smile.

*　　　*　　　*

It didn't take long for Guy to forget his disappointment at his friend's *no show*, and soon relaxed in the company of the red-headed dream that had joined his table. They laughed and joked over a number of drinks, and as the evening progressed he felt himself growing closer to her. Never had he felt such an unspoken connection with another human being; an attraction so strong he could almost see it crackle between them. As she spoke he watched her lusciously full lips move and imagined what it would be like to kiss them.

'I've not seen you round here before,' Guy enquired, wanting to know more about her.

'It's seasonal,' she answered. 'I'm around for the Christmas period then gone, just after the New Year.'

'Ahh, you must be a university student then,' he surmised.

'I'm a bit too old for that,' Dawn winked as she responded.

Removing her black cardigan, Guy caught sight of the tattoo that had previously intrigued him. Its fascinating pull had not waned.

'You see it's not a reindeer,' she laughed as she brought her arm closer to him, lifting the sleeve of her t-shirt so the design could be seen in its entirety.

Studying it in more detail, he saw the shape of a blue tree trunk, its branches spiralling from its centre. The pinks and reds showed flowers of cherry blossom hanging delicately from its natural weave, peppering the picture with star-shaped bursts of colour.

'That's a nice ink,' he smiled, feeling the effects of alcohol widen his grin.

'It's a reminder of my home,' she cooed softly. 'My heart.' Dawn giggled as she picked up her pint glass and changed the subject, 'I had an ex that reminded me of a reindeer once.'

'An ex?' Guy enquired.

'Yeah. He used to wear his hair in tufty spikes and his nose was always red. Some strange side effect from eating onions.'

'My hair's spikey,' Guy pointed out.

'Not like his,' she retorted. 'His was something else.'

Guy grew a little dejected.

Dawn caught sight of his body language.

'Don't go getting all jealous,' she assured him. 'He's an ex for a reason. But you're no reindeer. Look at you with your chest all puffed out trying to be the *big I am*. You're more like a robin.' Dawn laughed affectionately. 'My little robin red breast.'

'Can I sit in your tree?' Guy joked as he pointed to her tattoo; his smile returning.

He reached out and caressed her arm.

Did it move? Did he just see the branches sway? Had the cherry blossom danced delicately over the ripples of flesh, over the pulse of her blood and the ebb and flow of contracting muscles?

'You can sit in my tree, if you dare. But with all that red already in the branches the little robin red breast might disappear!' Her laughing slowly died down and she gulped back the last of her drink. 'Guy, I like you,' her tone grew serious. 'I'd like to show you something. Something very special to me. Will you come?'

His expression dropped to reflect hers.

'Of course. Now?' He looked at his watch, it read 23:15.

Maybe Christmas had come early.

*   *   *

12

Snowflakes gently danced in the night air, partnered by a retreating gale. Guy and Dawn had wrapped themselves up well in their coats, scarves and hats, keeping the winter temperatures at bay. Dawn's mitten held Guy's hand as she led him through the city centre and toward the park.

'Do you like poetry?' she asked as they continued on their journey, her breath like white smoke in the chill.

'I've read some,' Guy replied, a little ashamed he didn't know more than a handful of verses from school.

'I love poetry,' Dawn went on. 'The expression of words so beautifully placed capture my soul.' She paused for a moment, her tone turning wistful. 'But it has already been captured by something else.'

'What?'

'Sshhh… I want to show you.'

She smiled excitedly as the world around them shed the orange glare of the city's streetlights and instead they were bathed in the ethereal glow of the moon, reflecting on the snow that lay across the park's grassed surface.

'There,' she said stopping and pointing toward a bank of trees. 'Through there.'

Guy followed the direction of her finger, and as he walked further out he saw a small clearing past the bank. Stepping into the clearing, the light grew brighter as the moon's reflection intensified, engulfing the area in a silvery shimmer. At the centre of the ghostly glow, hidden from the park by all sides, stood a tree unlike any of those around it.

Despite the snow that had fallen and the winds that had blown, red leaves stubbornly gripped onto the end of its branches, refusing to let go.

There was less than twenty leaves on its whole canopy, but in contrast to its barren neighbours it was a spectacle of abundance and determination. The leaves shook in the gusts that threatened to take them, but resolutely they stayed firm.

'It looks like your tattoo,' Guy remarked, half to himself.

'It's beautiful,' Dawn caught up with him, her gaze focused on the tree. 'Its mere existence is the most majestic poem I have ever known, and truly it has my soul.'

'Why is it like this?' Guy asked, unable to take his eyes from the swaying branches as they writhed in the winds, conducting the swirl of snowflakes that continued to fall.

'It's the spirit of life. It clings on despite the harsh environment that surrounds it.' Dawn's voice seemed to trail off, no longer speaking to him, but voicing an inner thought deep inside of her. 'It refuses to die. It holds on. I admire its stubbornness.'

Walking closer, Guy made out the detail of the large trunk. It looked charred, as if it had been burnt long ago. Its girth was covered in moss and ivy, but between the creepers that grew on the bark he saw something else.

'There's a hole in the base,' he called back to her. 'It looks big enough to crawl in.'

The black shape on the tree was too dark and refused to give up its secrets. Even as Guy stood inches from it, he couldn't see beyond the veil of vines that covered the opening.

A hand took hold of his and pulled him back.

'Don't,' Dawn said softly and leant into him. 'Merry Christmas,' she whispered before gently placing her lips against his.

He pulled her closer as the passion in their kiss grew. Her tongue slid into his mouth, taking him by surprise. They both stumbled, and he felt his back land against the soft bark of the tree. Around them the wind howled, forcing the branches overhead to sway in a rhythm that matched their gyrating hips. Her crotch pressed against the swelling in his trousers and he smiled to feel the warm breath of her gasp as he softly kissed her neck.

Moving her hair to expose her sensuous nape, Guy slid his tongue over her soft skin. Dawn bit her lip in excitement. Her eyes widened as she felt the bulge between his legs, cupping his solid erection with one hand, the other hurriedly undid his buttoned fly, eager to feel the nakedness of his manhood.

Carefully pulling it from his boxer shorts, Dawn positioned his cock under her skirt, gently rubbing the helmet of his penis against her crotch; teasing her clitoris through the fabric of her tights.

'I want you,' she whispered, causing Guy to groan with excitement.

He heard a tear as she pulled at her tights, ripping a hole in the nylon between her legs. He felt the warmth of her thigh and the silk of her underwear, saturated from her soaking pussy.

Taking hold of his cock once more, Dawn slid her pants to one side and eased the length of his erection into the velvet wetness of her eager vagina.

She groaned as she felt his girth slowly fill her.

'Fuck, that's so good,' she moaned, lowering herself

further onto him.

They fell forward and Guy gripped her ass; her skirt now soaking from the snow, as he lay on top of her.

He thrusted, deep and hard.

'Without you I'm nothing,' she cried as she writhed on the floor beneath him, her eyes closed, concentrating on the ecstasy that ran through her. 'That's it, my little robin red breast. That's perfect.'

Dawn wailed as she approached climax, tracing her hands around his body, feeling the lines of the man that was doing all he could to please her.

'I am a husk,' she called through her growing screams of delight. 'Fuck me. Fill me.'

Guy bit his own lip in amazement as he felt Dawn's pussy tighten around his shaft.

The world began to spin around him. The wind turned to song as the darkness that surrounded the clearing roared to life with the echo of Dawn's euphoric shrieks.

Who was this girl?

She was so beautiful.

This sort of thing didn't happen to him.

He unzipped her coat and lifted her top, revealing her breasts whilst feeling the warmth of her flesh. Her touch felt so perfect, so right against his skin. His hips naturally fell along the curves of hers like two pieces of a jigsaw puzzle finding their place.

'You're so gorgeous,' he whispered, trying to find the words for the emotions he felt.

How could he convey these feeling?

His lips caressed hers as he thrust with increasing rhythm.

Was she his perfect match? His other half?

The wetter she grew the further he felt himself slide.

Gently holding her wrists, he pressed them to the ground, but froze when his fingers sunk into her flesh, pushing into the skin like it was soft wax. He left go, shocked to see his grip had misshapen her arms, leaving indents from his fingers like kneaded dough.

'Are you okay?' he asked in alarm.

'I need you,' she smiled as she took hold of him and pulled him closer, seemingly oblivious to the harm he'd caused.

Caught in her embrace, Guy felt his torso sink into something soft; something warm and wet. The moon's reflection had made them both look ghostly, but it provided enough light for him to see Dawn's body begin to change; to soften, turning into a strange gel beneath him. Slowly his chest was enveloped by the thick, stodgy substance that took the place of her once beautiful skin, and try as he might to fight it, it stuck to him like glue. With each attempted thrust and push, each vain bid to escape, he found himself sinking deeper and deeper into her.

'What's happening?' Guy called out, unable to comprehend the events unfolding before him.

'Sssshhhh, my darling,' she cooed.

Dawn's face twisted, her features falling into a puddled mess with a grotesque, watery grin as Guy sunk further.

'Stop your crying,' she continued. 'Without you I could no longer live.'

Pain shot up Guy's arms, and as he wrestled them free from the pink, bubbling goo, he screamed to find his hands missing; dissolved in the soft jelly of Dawn's unravelling body.

Blood sprayed from the end of his wrists. The grotesquely, gory stumps shot crimson geysers into the night air and peppered the snow several feet away, appearing almost luminous against the pure white.

Steam rose from his wounds into the cold as Guy watched, horrified to see his flesh dripping like melted ice cream down his arms. His skin poured like syrup, revealing corroding bones underneath that fizzed from the marrow.

Flailing in the swill of Dawn's changing torso, Guy found solid ground and dived towards it, rolling onto his back. Dawn followed suit, and her body, now more like a bubbling blancmange, rolled with him.

She straddled him, her form rapidly losing shape.

'What are you?' he cried, as the snow around him turned red.

Dawn's breasts slid down her body, falling like two giant globules of mucus-filled phlegm. They landed on Guy's chest exploding in an eruption of agony. The smell of burnt hair assaulted his nostrils as his ribs began to poke through his skin, weakened by the acidic-like contact of the girl above him and her liquid flesh.

Pleadingly he looked up to see Dawn's eyes illuminate with a fluorescent, light blue. Their unnatural luminescence shone out from her misshapen face, as gravity pulled at her features.

Tears flowed down his cheeks. 'What the fuck are you?!' Guy screamed.

He tried to get up, but the cruel glowing eyes fixed him to the spot, keeping him pinned as her warped features drew so close to his face he could taste her breath. Her chin oozed forward and dribbled on his, instantly burning the skin it touched.

'I'm the fairy in the tree,' she rasped. 'I'm your last Christmas.'

Her form gave up all human pretence as it collapsed into a giant puddle, washing over him and cutting his cries short as Gary was drenched with the fleshy porridge that was once her body. Gasping for air, he opened his mouth only for the soft tissue of his tongue to be immediately covered. Unable to articulate, he howled with primal fear as his tongue disappeared in a river of crimson that poured from his mouth, gushing down the ravaged remains of his chin.

A warped set of lips flashed a smiling set of teeth at him amongst the slime. They whispered hushed tones of sweet nothing and hummed an off-key Christmas carol as slowly Guy dissolved. His body liquefied as the scarlet colour of his blood mixed with the putrid puddle that surrounded him, until they became one indistinguishable entity, alone in the silent night.

*　　　　*　　　　*

Tom had his hands full of films as he made his way to the counter.

Christmas had given him a wealth of vouchers and the Boxing Day sales had been too good to resist. He smiled as he passed his haul of entertainment to the cashier. She was pretty and smiled politely, her full, red lips betraying an attraction.

Tom had always liked red-heads.

'Nice tattoo,' he said, looking for a way to start a conversation. 'That's a cute looking robin red breast.'

Christmas Wrath

The shovel was worn but still sturdy, burying deep into the face and almost slicing the head in two. Amid the slurping sound of squelching noises, he wiggled the tool free, then rammed it, with all his force, into the open gash he'd just made. As the top of the head separated from the rest and slopped to the floor, he laughed with a wicked grin.

'You see, Charlie. You've got to give it some real welly if want to do some damage,' the attacker sneered as he proudly instructed his young onlooker.

'Oi! What do you think you're doing?' An enraged voice called out from a bedroom window.

'Get bent, Grandma,' he called back, dropping the shovel on the snow-covered ground and laughing as he extended his middle toward the house. 'Your Grandson, *Tommy Twatface*, will just have to build you another snowman, you old crone.' Turning to his younger brother he whispered, 'And we'll come and knock that one over, right Charlie?'

Charlie nodded in agreement as they walked away from Mrs Patterson's front lawn and onto the snow-littered pavement. The roads had been salted but were still treacherous, making the town eerily quiet as commuters stayed at home, enjoying the rare occasion of a day snowed in from work.

At sixteen, Max was ten years older than his brother, and although he wasn't the biggest lad in his year, he was certainly one of the meanest. Life had been tough moving around from town to town, and he'd found it easier to put up a barrier of hatred than make friends, only to lose them when his Dad had another posting and they all had to move.

If they'd been in the forces there'd have been some kind of community, some kind of support network to fall back on, but there was no such privilege being a contract representative for Memory Inc. It was, however, a big deal. The family moved where they were required as the money was too good to refuse.

But none of this was an excuse for why Max was just so *mean*!

'Christmas is bollocks,' he told Charlie as they wandered down the street; his little brother doubling his steps in order to keep up with Max's lengthy strides. 'Snow, that's fucking bollocks. Presents, well okay presents are pretty good. But Father Christmas…?'

He left a pause and looked towards his brother.

'Bollocks?' Charlie said, unsure of his answer and hesitant to share in the profanities Max seemed to be revelling in.

'That's right,' Max smiled and patted the bobble hat on his brother's head as the pair wandered home.

*   *   *

'I can't believe he just said that!' Max's mother was a picture of disgust as she turned to her eldest in an accusatory fashion. 'What have you been teaching him?'

22

Charlie stood in the hallway biting his lip. The six year old had thought it was an innocent comment, something to carry on the conversation after dinner as they got ready to go back outside and head to this evening's carol service. From his mother's reaction he instantly realised he'd done wrong. Max had other ideas though.

'Yeah he said it, and he's right.' Max's defiance had been growing stronger with every passing year. 'I taught him it. Christmas is bollocks! You can drag Charlie along to the carol service if you like, but there's no way I'm going.'

'Maxwell Benjamin Saunders,' his mother protested, 'why must you insist on using such foul language? I've never spoken to you like that.'

'Not to my face,' he muttered.

'What was that?' she screamed, her patience finally pushed beyond its limit.

'Mum, I'm not going. Christmas is shit. The lights, the singing, the stupid decorations, the fake laughter and everyone pretending to get along. All of it is plain bullshit. The world is nothing more than a steaming pile of crap, and no one pretending otherwise is going to make any difference.'

'Have it your way,' his mother took Charlie's hand. 'This world is not perfect, and the winter nights can be depressing, especially when your father is away, but Christmas is a shining light in the middle of that blackness. It's a time for joy, and just because you don't want to have any part of it, don't ruin it for me and your brother!'

Holding back her tears she zipped up Charlie's coat,

kissed him on the cheek and left the house with her youngest in tow; mother and son disappearing into the night.

Max felt a shade of remorse as he watched them walk away. He pushed against his parents in everything they did, but they always remained supportive and caring. Today he'd seen a different side and a feeling of loneliness clawed at his soul. This was the first time she'd walked away. With his father away on business for a few days, then Charlie and his Mum abandoning him, the fear of solitary grew all-consuming.

'Fuck them,' he muttered to himself; his anger rising to his defence. 'Fuck them all.'

*   *   *

Max felt the burn from the last drops of vodka as he poured it down his throat.

With nothing to do and an anger to quench, he'd set out to the local retail park and hung around until he could cajole someone into buying him half a bottle of vodka and twenty cigarettes. He'd paid over the odds for both the supermarket's own brand of booze and a packet of Lambert & Butler, but at his age he was happy with what he could get.

Realising he'd left his keys in the house, he had no choice but to find somewhere to hang around until his family got back from the carol service. His wanderings had taken him along the river, under the bridge, a lap around the car park and across the cemetery.

Despite the alcohol in his bloodstream, Max began to feel the bite of the cold evening chilling his body. He threw the empty bottle against a headstone and smiled to hear it smash in the darkness.

The sound of Christmas carols filled the air as he made his way past the church. The rousing rhythm of *The Holly and The Ivy* faded into a gentle rendition of *Little Drummer Boy*. Max screwed up his face at the unashamedly joyful sounds.

Staggering towards the church he unzipped his flies and smiled as he relieved his bladder against the perimeter wall.

'This is my body,' he said as he waved his penis in the air, using his piss to draw over the crumbling stonework.

Standing back to admire the crude swastika he'd attempted to fashion with his urine, Max pulled a cigarette from his crumpled pack and lit the end. He sighed as he breathed in the sweet tasting smoke.

Undeterred and oblivious to his actions, the chorus carried on.

'Fucking sappy cunts,' he muttered as he scowled before slouching off, back towards the retail park.

People are pricks. And people that like Christmas, even more so!

Max's alcohol addled brain began amplifying his enraged thoughts.

Fuck Christmas! How dare they all be happy!

Without breaking his stride, the teenager launched his Doc Martin boot towards a garden gnome made up to look like Santa Claus. The hollow, clay model shattered on impact, littering the front garden it had stood in.

Max smiled, pleased with the satisfying feeling of destruction.

As he crossed the road towards the deserted retail

park he jumped up, grabbing hold of the overhead sign and swung on it, kicking out at the plastic reindeer that lined the entrance. As the plastic animals fell like dominoes he picked up the Rudolf and hurled it at the fake Father Christmas that sat proud at his sleigh.

The antlers careered into his face, cracking his cheeks and knocking his long, white beard to the floor. A crushing stamp of Max's boots saw both the beard of the old Saint and the smiling face of the most famous reindeer obliterated into tiny shards.

Not stopping there, Max caught hold of the fairy lights. Wrapping the wire around his hands, he pulled at them, tugging them from their fittings then running along the pedestrianised shop fronts, taking the lights down as he went.

Stopping to catch his breath, the teenager looked around for his next target. A twinkling snowman smiled at him through the window of Old Kitchen Italia, the town's finest Italian restaurant. The snowman's animatronic arm waved slowly at the boy and gave him a kitsch smile that riled his anger. This Disney-esque monstrosity was *exactly* what he hated about the over-camp holiday.

Looking around, Max spied a large plant in a pot and bent down to clasp it in his arms. Using all his strength, he picked up the shrub and aimed it at his target.

Swinging his hips backwards and forwards to build momentum, he counted in his head before hurtling the plant and its terracotta base towards the restaurant.

'Let it gooooo,' he sung in mock tunefulness as he watched the projectile crash through the window.

The plant pot cracked as it burst through the glass,

knocking the ornate snowman from its display stand and crashing through the net-curtain, landing unseen, somewhere in the restaurant with an almighty smash.

'What in the Lord's Mother Mary!' A gruff voice called out from inside the restaurant.

Max stumbled backwards, his legs buckling with fear. The voice was unexpected, the place had looked closed; deserted.

Lights came on, illuminating the restaurant's dining area amid a cacophonic commotion. Max heard more voices but he was unable to decipher what they were saying as their words fought over each other.

Three.

Four.

He couldn't work out exactly how many there were, and he didn't really care; his only thought was to escape.

Turning to run, his legs carried him before he'd even turned his head. When he did so, there was just enough time to see a large fist lined with misshapen knuckles come towards him.

Then everything went black.

*   *   *

His surroundings slowly emerged from the darkness, swaying with the motion of his still groggy head. Even when the images had settled down, he was at a loss to describe where he was, and it took a moment to remember the previous events.

It was only when that heavy fist, the one that had caused the swelling over his right eye, opened its palm and slapped him across the face to bring him back round

27

did he remember about the restaurant and the snowman.

Max found himself sat on a wooden chair in a small, dingy room, surrounded by three men in tailor-fitted suits. The walls were nothing more than exposed brickwork whilst a light bulb dangled from the centre of a poorly plastered ceiling. A large, chest freezer hummed in one corner of the room whilst a safe stood in another. Along the far wall was a battered old desk supporting a dusty computer and monitor. The keyboard was an off-white colour, and the screen flickered as it tried to keep its connection with the loose wiring at the back.

'So who the fuck is this chump?' a balding man enquired, stroking his well-groomed beard. 'Who sent you, you little shit?' he said as he leant in closer to Max and pulled the boy's hair back so their eyes met.

'I ain't got a clue,' said his ape-sized colleague with shovel-like hands; as hairy as they were large.

Max watched as he walked over to the freezer and opened the lid of the aged household appliance.

'Are you from the Kenzie's? Is that it?' The man with the beard gripped Max's jaw. 'What's the matter, you can't talk? Allow me to introduce myself. My name's Carlito John. Over there is Mumbo. You've already met his fists.' Carlito John chuckled a wheezing guffaw. 'Behind me is Muttz. You don't want to talk to Muttz. You think we're scary, you wait until you annoy Mr Muttz.'

Max's eyes darted from each person to the next. He's eyes lingered on the man named Muttz. He was much thinner than his two colleagues; his chin ending in a point that accentuated his goatee. His eyes were narrow and his cheek bones seemed so sharp they could cut the fingers of an errant caress. The pair locked eyes for a moment, and slowly Muttz's grin widened.

'You've been sent from Hamish, haven't you?' Muttz's softly spoken tone sent a chill down the boy's back.

'No,' Max cried, shaking his face free from the clutches of Carlito John. 'I haven't been sent by anyone.'

'Bullshit!' Carlito John's breath smelt of garlic, causing Max to turn his head as he tried to back away from his inquisitor.

'I swear!' Tears began to trace down the teenager's face. 'I was just messing around.'

'Oh, I see.' Carlito John's voice echoed insincerity. 'You did it for kicks, right? You fucked this place up *for kicks*! You can't come in here and bust up my Momma's restaurant and expect to get away with it! Only a fool would call that fun. Hey Mumbo,' Carlito John began laughing as he turned to the hulking gangster, 'this kid did it for kicks. He broke the window, smashed the decorations and ruined our dinner, JUST FOR KICKS! Mumbo, give me a fucking stick.'

Lifting his hands out of the freezer, Mumbo revealed what he had been searching around for. In his grip, wrapped in rag, was a long, cylindrical piece of ice. From base to tip it was approximately twelve inches in length, ending with a sharp point. Mumbo handed the rag and the ice to his boss.

Carlito John admired the weapon for a moment before turning to Max. 'Now I don't believe that you're telling the truth. Only an absolute imbecile would be vandalising my property, especially when there's supposed to be a truce at Christmas. You're gang

29

material, kid. I can see it running through you. The question is, what's the name? We're going to find out.' His smile widened as his eyes darkened with malice. 'I have before me a piece of ice, nothing more, nothing less. This piece of ice, as you can see, is moulded to end in a point. In fact the whole thing looks like a very large pin. And just like a pin, it's very, very sharp.

'I can, and I will, push this piece of ice through your body. Where shall I do it? Your knee? Your cheek? Your ass? How about in your eye?' He sighed with delight as he reminisced about a memory his last statement had triggered. 'You might be thinking that the cold ice might help numb the pain, but it won't. You might think that the sharpness of the point will make a clean incision, but it won't. In fact the more I sit here talking, the more the point begins to melt, causing it to blunt, meaning I'm gonna have to work really hard to force the fucker in.'

Max squirmed in his seat. He wanted to stand up and run, but Mumbo had rested his hand on the teenager's shoulder warning him of his watch over the captive boy.

'Mumbo, hold the boy still,' Carlito John ordered.

Compliant as always, Mumbo did as he was instructed, gripping the boy's face and forcing his left eye wide. Max struggled in Mumbo's hold, trying his hardest to break free, but it was too little, too late.

Aiming the length of the frozen rod at Max, Carlito John slowly brought the point to his face. Clumsily the tip scratched against the teenager's cheek, before it came closer, brushing against his eyelashes. Max blinked in an involuntary effort to keep the point at bay, but it was already inside the protective boundary of the boy's natural defenses. Too scared to fight them off in case any sudden movements pushed it closer, all he could do was sit still and pray for a miracle as his skin grew cold from the presence of the makeshift torture device.

He prayed for help. He prayed to God, to his Dad, to Father fucking Christmas.

This could not be happening.

Hope deserted his thoughts as Max's tear duct streamed with water. The ice spike scraped against the lens of his eyeball, making a sound that reverberated through his head, forcing his teeth to grind in sympathy. He felt the weight of the weapon push against his eye, altering its oval shape and forcing it gently back into his skull.

He could sense the lens about to give way. The eyeball had reached its maximum point of stress. Any more pressure and penetration was guaranteed. The soft outer layer would burst, folding itself around the end of the spike and a dark grey liquid would pour from the wound, inciting a burning agony, like nothing he'd ever felt before.

Carlito John licked his lips as he indulged in the anticipation.

He squeezed the rag, wrapped round the ice spike, a little harder and gently increased the force.

'What the hell is going on in here?' A female voice, high-pitched and enraged, erupted from somewhere the other side of the darkened doorway. 'What the hell happened to my beautiful snowman?!' The tone changed to one of sadness as her voice quivered.

A short lady, around sixty-five with deep, olive skin entered the room. Her grey hair was tied up in a headscarf, her slippers encased her feet in a fluffy pattern of pinks. Her matching dressing gown did the same to her body.

'I'm sorry, Momma,' Carlito John pulled the piece of ice from Max's face and turned to face his distraught mother. 'I'm fixing it.'

'You're fixing what?' she cried. 'And what are you doing to little Maxwell Saunders?' she asked, turning to see the boy.

'You know this kid?' her son asked.

'I know everyone round here. It's my business. I don't know him very well, but I've seen him. He's a tearaway. Reminds me of you when you were little. Got the same cheeky smile and chubby cheeks.'

She gripped her son's face and gave it a playful squeeze.

'Momma,' Carlito John laughed playful, 'leave it out, will you?'

'This is Max, he's the son of Craig Saunders,' she continued. 'You know, the computer guy you had here the other day.'

'You know my dad?' Finally Max found the courage to speak again.

'Saunders is muling for us this weekend,' Muttz reminded his boss. 'Would be pretty off to hurt his kid whilst he's away doing a job for us.'

'But he works for Memory Inc?' Max protested.

'Course he does, boy,' Carlito John smiled. 'But life is expensive. Especially when you've got a wife and two kids to feed. Sometimes you've got to make a little extra dough. I rarely ever seen a father so committed to his family. He could almost pass for Italian.'

'So what we gonna do with the kid, boss?' Mumbo

asked.

'He can't go unpunished,' Carlito John replied, his mind trailing off into thought. 'He can't come round and fuck up my Momma's restaurant and get away unscathed. I have to send out a message.'

He grimly smiled as an idea formed.

*   *   *

Max sat shivering on his parent's front lawn. He'd been there for an hour; told to kneel on the ground whilst the gangsters tied his hands and feet. They'd encased him in snow, surrounding his body until he was no longer visible, except for a head poking out the top of a huge mound.

Carlito John had laughed as he firmly stuck a piece of duct tape over the teenager's mouth, ensuring his silence whilst he was forced to wait it out in the cold.

'Quit your whining, you little prick,' Muttz had said as he'd placed the ornamental head of the snowman – the one Max had broken – over the boy's exposed face. 'Your family will be back soon. You ain't gonna die out here.'

'But whilst you wait,' Carlito John chipped in, 'think about what happens when you fuck with me and my family. If it wasn't for your dad being such a good man you'd be looking at us with only one eye.'

Max could barely see out from the helmet-like head of the snowman; a few small cracks had given him a hampered glimpse of the three men that stood around him. Their voices echoed inside the bowl of the ornate head, making them sound as if they were speaking underwater.

'Don't freeze your bollocks off,' Mumbo had chuckled, prompting the others to laugh with him as they'd walked away. 'It'd be a shame to lose them before you ever knew what they're for.'

Their callous laughter was the only sound he'd heard beside his chattering teeth in the last hour, and it continued to loop in his mind, round and round.

The revelation about his father working for the gangsters danced through his thoughts. How long had his father being doing these dodgy deals? And how far was he prepared to go to keep his family in pocket? A strange kind of respect began to form. Max couldn't remember the last time his Dad ever said *no* to him about anything. It was Max who was the one always challenging, arguing, not the other way round.

He'd always been given his own way, and never once did he spend Christmas day without exactly what he'd asked for, and more.

The taste of roast potatoes and gravy tickled his tongue as he remembered back to Christmas when he was younger. They were fun times, and his parents always made sure the day was packed with laughter and joy. They still did.

A tear rolled down his cheek as he remembered waking up early in the morning to feel the weight of a stocking full of gifts on his bed. How he and Charlie would quietly open their presents so as not to wake Mum and Dad. Of course their giggling would soon put paid to the stealth approach, but neither adult minded, and before long it was mince pies for breakfast and a house that smelt divine with a turkey in the oven.

He'd have done anything to be there again. To be wrapped up in the love of his family. If only he'd gone to the carol service and got into the spirit of the season. All that love was still there waiting for him, he just had to accept it.

A remorseful sigh escaped his body. He was sorry for being such a brat. Yes, life was hard, but he didn't have to be such an asshole to those he loved. He wanted to pull crackers, eat sprouts and play board games with his family. He wanted to sit in a room with the lights out and watch the Christmas tree twinkle whilst he told his brother stories of how he nearly caught Santa Claus coming down the chimney. He wanted to hear his brother laugh in that innocent way that can only come from a child.

His inner turmoil was given a reprieve as he heard the sounds of footsteps approaching.

'Oh look, a snowman,' Max heard his mother call in delight. 'Maxwell must have made it.'

He watched the two figures walk past him. A jingle of the keys and a burst of light from the hallway signalled his mum had entered the house.

'Max?' he heard her call.

Max tried to call back, but the tape had him silenced. He shuffled his shoulders and tried to barge out of his snowy cocoon, but his tormentors had packed him in tight. With his weakened body using all its energy to keep him warm he had no strength left to push past the frozen wall.

'Max!' she called again. 'Strange. He must have popped out. Still nice to see him getting into the Christmas spirit. What do you think of the snowman,

Charlie?'

'I love it,' Charlie replied.

'I'll run you a bath,' she said to her youngest. 'You can play in the snow for a few moments whilst I fill up the tub.'

Max watched his mother disappear into the house. He called again trying to attract the attention of his brother. He groaned as loud as he could, desperate to carry a sound past his gag.

Charlie stopped playing and gazed back, curiously.

Good man, Charlie. You've heard me!

Max's heart quickened, excited at the possibility of escape.

Slowly Charlie wandered towards him. Max shifted his view inside the ceramic head, trying to get a better look at his brother.

What was that he had in his hand?

A spade?

What did he have a spade for?

Good God, no!

Charlie had learnt well from watching his older brother.

Using all his might, the shovel buried deep into the snowman's face, crunching bone and porcelain alike as it sliced through the head and split Max's skull. Not being as strong as his brother, it took Charlie four more attempts before he successfully forced the rusty tool all the way through; finally separating the head from the rest of the body.

He didn't notice the red snow as he revelled in his act of destruction; laughing, just as his brother had, as the broken remains slopped to the floor.

A Christmas Tradition

Kerry was dying.

Upstairs in the attic room of her parents' house, she surveyed what was once her childhood bedroom, surrounded by boxes piled higher than she was tall. The young woman did her best to block out the sounds that filled the house, but the screaming was relentless and made her stomach pull tight. Bile climbed her throat in revulsion, leaving a caustic taste that filled her airwaves.

Why did they do it?

Why did they commit these vile acts of torture?

Every year the same video was brought out.

The one of her in the choir.

Barely in primary school and dressed as an angel, she was caught on camera singing with her school friends in her first Christmas concert. Kerry didn't need a video to remember the white gown, coat hanger wings and a tinsel halo framing a bowl-like haircut. *That* haircut was proof her parents hated her. There was no other explanation. And the same hate seemed to continue to this day, embarrassing her and anyone that was willing to watch the film, as Kerry's over-eagerness had seen her screaming Christmas carols at the top of her lungs. Her voice drowned out all others with an accent steeped in her Bristol upbringing; a true west-country, farmer-like twang flavouring her words.

God, she hated them for doing this.

Away in a Manager, Little Donkey, We Three Kings.

At twenty-four she'd thought this embarrassment would be buried; lost in time. The grainy VHS tape with the label *Kerry at Christmas* however, offered no such solace. Every year it would appear. And every year she would grow red and sulk in her old childhood bedroom, looking through the various boxes of old toys and keepsakes her parents had horded. At times like this she was thankful they were unable to throw anything away. This was where the real treasures from her youth could be found, and every year she'd go through a different box or two, searching for forgotten pieces of her past.

But try as she might, this distraction was never fully effective at blocking out the mental anguish. Even up the spiral staircase, right at the top of the house, Kerry could still hear her younger self unknowingly ruining her Christmases forever.

The tuneless cacophony of I Saw Three Ships knotted her stomach.

The embarrassment was killing her.

Kerry was dying.

Refusing to listen anymore she tried her best to absorb herself in her task and opened up another box.

'Oh cool, Robin Hood,' she said, hoping that talking aloud would help keep her focused.

She smiled as she looked over the familiar DVD cover, an image of a cartoon fox she'd seen so many times as a child, but one she'd not thought about in a long time.

The best Disney film, she told herself. *Much better than all that princess crap.*

Another box revealed a Barbie doll and her collection of Sylvanian families. The miniature, animal figurines were once cherished items, and even now she regarded them with fondness. But it was when she opened a third box, one she retrieved from the bottom of a stack, that a long forgotten memory came flooding back. Inside was a blue dress, an item of clothing that she'd loved, and one she vividly remembered wearing one particularly magical Christmas. It had been cold and the snow had settled outside on Christmas Eve. She wasn't much older than she'd been in the video.

Holding the tiny garment up and viewing it in the light, she allowed herself a small smile.

Looking back in the cardboard box she found a Quality Street tin that had been hidden underneath. The metal box of chocolates had no doubt been emptied of its sugary treats a long time ago, but Kerry had an inkling of what might be inside. Picking up the scratched and battered tin, she took some time to find the edge of the packaging tape that sealed the lid.

A bit overkill wasn't it? she wondered, before thinking back to how awfully her Dad wrapped presents.

Eventually finding the end, Kerry picked it at with her nails, teasing out enough of a strip to grip between her fingers and pull it free.

Opening the lid, a musty smell hit her. It was the aroma of old clothes that caused her nose to wrinkle in disgust, but nothing could wipe the growing grin from her face as she stared at the contents inside.

His fur was a little dusty and his button eyes were scratched, but his face beamed back at her as if the two had never been parted.

Scribbles!

She picked up the teddy and hugged it close to her cheek just as she had done all those years ago. Elated with her find, she held him at arm's length and admired his scruffy fur. Ruffling the large, round ears that sat on top of his head, Kerry sighed for a time gone by. She kissed him on the cheek then carefully put the toy back into the tin, placing it aside for safe keeping.

Excited by her find, and willed on to search out the next discovery, she dipped her hands back into the cardboard box, searching for more artefacts from her history. A loud crashing sound caused her to stop. Turning around, the tin had gone! Standing over the staircase she peered down its spiralling descent and caught sight of the overturned tin lying on the floor. The lid rattled against the wall of the landing as it finished rolling and came crashing to a stop.

Running down the stairs, Kerry almost fell, jumping the last few steps to keep her balance. Picking up the tin she turned it over, only to find it empty. A warped reflection of herself stared back from the shiny insides, startling her as she dropped the container. Kerry scanned the landing, but the floor was bare; Scribbles was nowhere to be seen!

'Oh dear, what's happened here?' her Mum said, ascending the stairs and noticing the upturned tin.

'I'm sorry Mum, I found it in a box. It had Scribbles in. You remember Scribbles?'

'That rascally bear.' Her face was soft with kindness as she picked up the chocolate container.

'I've lost him somewhere, can you help me look?'

'Come down!' her Dad called from the living room. 'It's your favourite part. They're just starting the nativity.'

'Oh really?' Kerry was not impressed.

'I'll look for him later,' her mother muttered as she smiled and headed back down to watch the video of her daughter proclaiming that a child of God is born.

She still had hold of the tin as she made her way back to the living room, marvelling at the memories it unleashed.

Kerry scanned the landing again.

Where could he be?

'Mu-' she went to call her mum again but was silenced before she could finish her first word.

A hand reached from behind and gripped her mouth, sealing it shut.

'Be quiet, child. Don't make a sound,' a voice whispered into her ear.

Kerry tried to break free of their grasp but the stranger overpowered her; keeping their hand clamped across her face whilst gripping her arm and holding the startled young woman close.

'You shouldn't have opened that tin.'

'Mmm-mm-phuf-mm,' Kerry tried to speak.

'Don't make a sound,' the stranger repeated, making it sound like a threat. 'We don't know where it's hiding.'

Her captor's breath was warm against her ear, and there was something familiar about their voice. She recognised it, but couldn't quite place it.

Kerry tried to resist again, but a blood-curdling shriek, like the screeching of a braking bus, halted her struggle. Fear gripped her body, weakening her legs and momentarily sapping her strength.

'Quickly we must go,' the voice instructed with an air of panic; releasing Kerry and turning to her.

'Grandma?' she sounded shocked as she looked at the kindly but concerned face of an old lady.

More cries echoed around the house, drowning out the familiar singing from the video.

The pair ran to the stairs, but halted as their path was blocked. Rising in front of them stood her teddy bear, Scribbles. Only it wasn't Scribbles. The bear was malformed: stretched and pulled so it stood almost seven feet tall. Its arms and legs were overtly long and beanpole thin, no longer wrapped in the cuddly texture of a soft toy's fur coat. This creature's skin was bare and taut, covering sinewy limbs. Its mouth opened to reveal a set of mismatched teeth, they were jagged and angular; all different sizes and protruding from its maw like broken metal rods. The once scratched button eyes had enlarged to the size of dinner plates, giving a blank stare that was as terrifying as it was emotionless. Even in the well-lit surroundings of the landing, they glowed with a ferocious intensity.

It roared again as it lashed out, swiping at them with one of its oversized claws.

They both jumped back, but its razor sharp talons caught the old lady's side.

'Follow me,' her Grandma ordered, gritting her teeth through the pain as she took Kerry by the hand and ran into the bathroom.

Locking the door behind her, the old lady looked around at her surroundings.

'Shit,' she exclaimed, gripping her bleeding waist.

'Wrong room.'

'What…?' Kerry couldn't find the strength to finish the sentence; confusion and fear mixed within her to form a debilitating cocktail.

'We must be quiet,' her Grandma whispered trying hard to calm her panic. 'That *thing* isn't your bear. It's not Scribbles. The demon has him now.'

'Demon?'

A muffled roar bounced off the bathroom tiles. The door rattled on its hinges and the sounds of grunting and snuffling filtered through from the other side of the woodwork.

The pair leant against the door, trying their best to keep the beast from compromising their barricade.

'Yes, my child,' her Grandma continued once she was satisfied she had her shoulder as hard to the door as she could. 'A demon. It came for you one day. We don't know why. No one could offer us an explanation. No one could tell us why it had to be you.' A tear formed in her eye as she was reminded of a fearful past. 'All we knew is it wouldn't stop. It just kept coming.'

Kerry felt the door shake, almost knocking her from her feet. Startled at first, she pushed back harder, determined to keep the monster at bay.

'But why don't I remember any of this?' she asked, perplexed at this new information about her past.

'You were young. You must have blocked it out.'

'But you stopped it?' Kerry asked.

'We didn't stop it, exactly,' her Grandma replied, 'we just kept-'

The old woman was cut off mid-sentence as the demon's claws burst through. She fell to the floor as the thing that was once loveable old Scribbles forced its way into their sanctuary and leapt on top of Kerry's Grandma.

Kerry tried to beat the monster away, but was thrown to the landing. The creature greedily licked its lips before sinking its misshapen teeth into the old lady's shoulder. She howled in pain as blood sprayed across the bathroom tiles. Another savage maul saw her left arm severed at the elbow. The demon's mouth dripped with crimson liquid as it dug its claws into the soft wrinkled skin of her back. The pensioner writhed under the beast, kicking and screaming in agony, but the monster was too powerful.

Climbing to her feet, Kerry was numb with shock as she watched the atrocity unfold before her eyes. Her Grandma turned to face her.

'Run, my dear,' the old lady's voice gargled in her own blood. 'Run!'

Kerry stood on shaky legs and bolted for the stairs, but the creature was already hot on her tail. Leaving the old woman to slowly bleed out, the demon hunched on to all fours and galloped towards her like a charging grizzly. Feeling her pursuer gaining, Kerry knew she had no chance of making it to the stairs before it caught her. She had to find cover. She had to get something between her and it.

Diving into her parents' bedroom she slammed the door, but the monster demolished it as if it was hardly there.

Trapped and cornered Kerry desperately searched for a way out. She tried the window, but her unsteady hands shook with adrenaline and failed to grip the latch enough to pull the lock from its fitting. Instinctively she bolted towards another door, ran through it and slammed it shut behind her.

Sinking her to knees, Kerry held her breath. In the darkness of the wardrobe she could do nothing but wait and listen to the drumming of her own heart. It filled her thoughts as she hid between the hanging contents of coats and dresses.

The stillness was broken by a nerve-shredding scream. She recognised it as the monster's. It howled and yelped, before the sound of its canter grew fainter and more distant.

Kerry didn't know what to do, and so for a moment she remained motionless, listening out for signs of the demon whilst trying to catch her breath. A fear-dried throat made it difficult to swallow and her pulse refused to slow.

Carefully, she opened the wardrobe and peered around the door. The bedroom floor was covered in fragments left in the aftermath of the demon's destructive rampage; wood chips and splinters littering the carpet.

Kerry wanted to shout, to call out to her parents and warn them of the danger but she was too terrified the thing might come back.

Where had it gone?

Kerry gently closed the wardrobe and caught sight of her reflection in its outer mirrored surface. *Was that what had made the monster scream and run? Its own reflection?*

She thought back to where she found it. In the Quality Street tin. The insides were reflective, forcing the demon to stare at its own image no matter which way it turned.

Was that how they'd kept it contained? Trapped and subdued by the hellish vision of its own horrific self?

Tip-toeing across her parents' bedroom, Kerry looked into the hallway. Huge, red marks – bloodied paw prints – tracked across the beige shag pile, circling around the landing then heading downstairs.

Good God, no!

The sound of the worn VHS tape was still blaring from the living room. A child explained there was no room at the Inn.

Nervously edging down each step in turn, Kerry glanced back and forth, expecting the demon to launch from its hiding place at any moment. She tried her best to avoid gazing into the bathroom, but her stomach turned as her eyes couldn't help but lock on to the ravaged pile of meat that was once her Grandmother.

Terror held back her tears, stifling her grief as she continued her descent.

Creeping across the hallway, she followed the footprints as they trailed along the passage then turned towards the living room.

Holding her breath, Kerry clung to the door frame and edged round it to get a clearer look.

The television flickered with the grainy footage of a group of children stood on a stage with tea towels on their heads. A baby doll lay in a wooden crib as the children stood round; three presenting the pretend parents with gifts.

Her own parents were sat in their usual armchairs nonchalantly watching the home video.

Had they not heard all the commotion?

Did the volume of the film really drown all that out?

Kerry scanned around for the bear but the room looked devoid of its demonic presence. The footprints stopped at the door. *Did it just disappear?*

A low rumble above her head told her exactly where the monster was.

Looking up, she had just enough time to see it clinging to the ceiling – its claws dug firmly into the plaster – before it launched itself at her.

Diving out of its way, Kerry fell into the living room, landing between her parents and the television.

'Mum, Dad. You've got to run!' she screamed.

Her parents ignored her, glued to the nostalgic images on the screen.

The beast rose on its hind legs and gripped the door frame, lowering its head to make it through the entrance. It snarled as it regarded its prey. Drool dripped from between its misaligned, jutting teeth; the tusk-like canines glinting in the glow of the television.

Kerry tried to climb to her feet and make a break for it, but the demon lurched forward, striking her face with one of its claws. She fell to the ground, her face pouring blood as it streamed from the gashes across her cheek. She watched the claret coloured liquid drip onto the floor as she fought the dizzy aftermath of the sudden attack.

Forcing herself to her feet, she span round trying to keep her balance. The monster swiped at her belly. Its claws raked through her flesh, opening up her stomach.

She fell backwards and held her wounds, trying to stop the blood gushing from her body.

Looking up at her parents she was shocked to see

them still impassively sat in the same positions.

'Mum,' she called as the demon stood over her.

Its big eyes, like headlights from a bus, peered down at her. The monster hunched on all fours, lowering its head so it was only inches away from the wounded woman.

'Help me!' Kerry called out, but her parents didn't move. Their eyes looked through the pair, trained on the television.

As the monster sunk its teeth into her side a glinting object caught her gaze.

Instinctively, she kicked out, pushing the monster away for a moment; giving her enough time to turn and see what was flashing in her peripheral vision. It was the Quality Street tin!

Wounded she may be, but now she'd found her weapon; the same one her Grandma must have used all those years ago. The tide was turning. The beast could be trapped!

Reaching out she stretched for the tin. Her fingers caught hold of the metal container just as a claw struck her arm. The attack sliced through her bicep, severing bone and flesh alike.

The tin fell to the floor splashing in a pool of blood, followed by the vomit-inducing thud as her separated limb did the same.

Kerry stared at her still-twitching hand; shock reducing the pain to a numbing buzz that filled her head.

Turning to face her attacker she watched as another swipe of its lethal claw came flying towards her, raking at her jaw. It destroyed the lower part, snapping it in two across the gum line and tearing it from her face. Kerry tried to call out but her tongue swung uselessly beside the hanging fragments of skin and teeth that remained of her mouth.

Blood bubbled up from her throat as the monster roared with a terrifying sound like that of screeching tyres. Its skin shone red and its breath smelt like diesel. Its headlight eyes shone brighter the closer they grew. Burning rubber filled the air and the sound of screaming passengers reminded her of snow. She looked down to see she was wearing her favourite blue dress, the one she'd found in the attic. Her back felt cold as snow soaked her skin, and Scribbles looked up at her, the faithful toy clutched in her hand.

Kerry closed her eyes, unable to watch as the blood splattered demon reached back and struck once more, aiming for her throat; the final death blow.

Gasping for breath, she felt the warmth of her own blood as it poured down her neck.

Unable to fill her lungs with air, she watched the room around her grow dark.

Kerry was dying.

Janet Francis picked up the Quality Street tin and placed it back on the coffee table.

'Must be the ghost,' her husband half-joked.

'Oh come now, don't be stupid,' she retorted.

'How else do you explain it?' Jeff asked. 'Every year it's always the same when we put the video on. Every Christmas the tin and the bear. How else do you explain all that banging around?'

'Pipes,' Janet replied. 'Pipes and false hope. Our baby was taken away from us at such an early age.'

'Your sister said she saw her here once,' he cut in.

'My sister has always been a bit of a fruit-loop,' Janet rebuffed his comment. 'Anyway she said she saw a woman in her twenties.'

'Maybe ghosts age. I don't know how it works.' Jeff sat back and thought for a moment, stroking his chin as he allowed his mind to drift. 'She'd be about that age now.'

'Twenty–four,' Janet cut in, slightly hurt that her husband hadn't known the answer instantly.

He relaxed back in his chair, allowing the comfort of the luxurious upholstery to envelop his shoulders as he snacked on an After Eight mint.

'Maybe you should have buried the bear with her. She was holding it when the bus… well, you know.'

'Maybe I should have,' Janet snapped, wiping the collecting grief from her eyes. Even after all these years the pain of losing her six year old daughter in a motor accident had not dulled. 'But it was her most treasured toy. Do you remember that Christmas? The snow? I wanted to keep that memory.' She paused for a moment, holding a thought of comfort in her head. 'Our little girl is in heaven now.'

'You're right,' Jeff could sense the growing agitation in his wife, and was happy to steer the conversation to more comforting territory. 'Your mother loved her so much. She'll be up there, keeping an eye on her.'

'Hush now,' Janet spoke, her voice soft and calming as she focused on the choir as they prepared for their grand finale. 'I want to watch this. I want to remember my beautiful daughter.'

Black Aura

'Control, this is Black Aura.'

Aron Buckhard sat back in the pilot's chair and smiled as he adjusted his headset, noisily chewing on a piece of gum.

'Nice of you to join us, Captain,' an irritated, female voice buzzed through his headphones.

'Hey, come on, it's Christmas Eve,' he replied.

'Exactly. So you know how important today is.'

Aron looked out the cockpit window at the hoses connected to the fuselage.

'I can't be late,' he answered back, his cheeriness not dampened by the annoyance from Control. 'The tankers are still filling up the juice.'

'Aron,' Control sighed, admitting defeat in the face of his arrogance, 'you can be a real prick sometimes.'

'You love me really,' he laughed and pulled the gum out of his mouth, sticking it to the dashboard.

Looking out across the runway, he watched the last remaining rays of light wink out existence as the sun disappeared behind the horizon. *Another Christmas Eve run*, he thought as he smiled and checked the dials in front of him before glancing over his shoulder and watching the tankers pull away, taking the disconnected hoses with them.

British Airways, he noted as he glanced at the insignia

on the wing tip. *We're flying classy today.*

A noise from behind interrupted his thoughts, making him turn and glance around, into the plane. His mouth dropped as the pilot watched the slender figure of a woman walk towards him, his eyes hypnotised by the graceful way she sauntered down the aeroplane. Her long legs caught his breath as she delicately balanced on a set of stiletto heels. The woman removed her hat and allowed her light, brown hair to fall, hanging in gentles waves that rested on her shoulders, almost obscuring the British Airways logo on her lapel. Sitting in the chair next to him, she glanced over, her ruby-red lips forming a smile and her eyes sparkling from the reflection of the strip lights that began lighting up the airfield.

'Control,' Aron spoke into his headset, not once taking his eyes off his co-pilot. 'Control, I'd just like to express my sincere gratitude to the recruitment department. I was told my new partner was going to be female, but you've outdone yourselves.'

'Hi I'm Yvonne,' the woman said, leaning forward and holding her hand out in a friendly gesture.

'Hello, Yvonne,' Aron said with enthusiasm as he shook her hand. 'Welcome aboard the Black Aura. I'm Captain Buckhard. But you can call me Aron.'

'Pleased to meet you, Aron.' Her smile grew wider. 'And a pleasure to be flying with you today.'

The pair turned to face forwards as the Captain started up the plane. Heading towards the runway, clearance was given by Control and they accelerated, picking up speed and taking off. All the while Aron watched Yvonne from the corner of his eye, taking sly moments to glance at her shapely legs. He felt his trousers bulge as he imagined placing his hands on her ass and sliding the fitted, blue skirt up over her thighs to reveal a pair of stockings.

'Eve, are you single?' Aron asked.

'Keep your mind on the job, Captain,' she smirked as she answered.

Clearing his throat in an attempt to change his tone, he did his best to ignore the rejection. 'We've got a full sweep to perform tonight,' he briefed with a sense of seriousness. 'We don't normally do the whole country in one evening, but Christmas Eve is a little different.'

That'll show her who's boss around here, he thought to himself as he let a subtle smile influence his expression.

'Doesn't it bother you?' Yvonne asked.

'Bother me?' he countered, slightly taken aback by the question.

'Doing this job?' she continued. 'Spraying the population like this. Hosing them down with mind-control chemicals.'

'Nah.' Aron leant back in his chair.

'But you're responsible for keeping them docile and compliant.' Anger began to bubble in her tone. 'I mean it's not just them is it? It's all of us. You're getting effected by the chemicals too.'

'Maybe,' he answered with an air of ambivalence. 'But why should I care? I get a fantastic pay packet, long holidays and a cool uniform that the chicks dig. I'm also one of the few pilots that doesn't have to put up with the irritation of actual passengers; present company excluded.' He winked. 'All I have to do is fly over the country and flick a switch.'

'But you're being controlled,' she turned to him. 'The

spray, it's changing your mood. Influencing your decisions. Modifying your behaviour!'

'And?' he snorted. 'I'm happy with my life. I'm good looking, I have a big dick and I get paid a lot of money. If I'm being controlled, so what? I have everything I need. Listen sugar-lips, if you have a problem with this whole set up then you're in the wrong job.'

He checked the altitude dial and glanced at the clock.

'We'll head to the top of the country, then down and up, and back home again in time for a Christmas breakfast, some champagne and a hot tub. You're welcome to join me.' Aron glanced at his new co-pilot, but received no favourable response from his invitation. 'Start to level out, and when we see the city lights of Sheffield, flick the switch.'

*   *   *

Inhaling deeply on a cigarette, Aron pulled up his trousers, closed the toilet lid and flushed the chain. He sat back down on the sealed seat as the toilet gurgled beneath him, cursing himself for his lack of success hitting on his new co-pilot. She was incredible. An absolute knock out. Normally they were putty in his hands, but Yvonne seemed resistant to his charms.

He exhaled just as slowly as he had breathed the smoke in, and fantasised that she was knelt in front of him; her lips pursed and hungry to slide round his cock.

Damn she looked good in that uniform!

The Aura Ops had chosen well with British Airways tonight. They had to disguise their crafts as a different airline each time they flew so the conspiracy theorists wouldn't twig it was the same set of planes. Sometimes it was Ryan Air, Emirates, Air Canada; it didn't matter. It seemed today he'd been given an early Christmas present. God, he loved that uniform.

The conspiracy theorists were right of course: *chem trails* they called them. A stupid name, but they'd hit the nail on the head when they figured out the origin and purpose of the cloud-like streaks in the sky. Mind control. Nothing drastic, he was told. Just to ensure a little more compliance; like the fluoride in the water supply.

Finishing his cigarette, Aron stood up and lifted the toilet seat, throwing the cigarette butt into the bowl before letting the lid slam.

He wasn't going to give up. He deserved a decent Christmas after all his hard work, and Yvonne was just the Christmas he wanted. Opening the door to the cubicle he walked through the empty plane. The chemical tanks took up a lot of the plane's interior, but there was still plenty of room inside. The sound of the engines hummed in the dimly lit space. There was no need for it to be any brighter, no need for an array of light fittings when there were no passengers on board. Stopping to look out the window at the peaceful darkness, a thought slowly dawned on Captain Buckhard: Why was it so dark?

Not inside the plane.

Outside.

They should be over Sheffield by now. The glowing lights of the city should be shining from below. And where was the sound of the spray tanks releasing their cargo? As pleasing as the gentle throb of the engines were, it should have been obscured by the hiss of four high pressured hoses.

Aron went to call out to his co-pilot, to find out what in the blazes was going on, when a banging caught his attention. A loud thud echoed from his left. Following the direction of the sound, the Captain reached out and turned the handle of a storage cupboard. As the door swung open a mop fell to the floor, making him jump back.

Tumbling out, after the cleaning appliance, was the body of a woman, bound by rope, gagged with duct tape and stripped to her underwear.

Landing in an unflattering heap on the floor, the woman looked towards him with tear-stained eyes.

'What the fuck?' he muttered, but didn't have a chance to think any further.

He instantly froze when he heard the unmistakable click of a gun hammer being pulled into position.

'Don't you fucking move,' Yvonne commanded as she stood by the door to the cockpit, both hands steadying a revolver that pointed at Captain Buckhard.

'Eve?' Aron slowly turned to face her. 'Babe, what's going on?'

'Don't call me that, you ignorant shit,' she demanded, her tone venomous and uncaring. 'This plane has been taken over by the Anti-Illuminati Initiative.'

'Eve. Yvonne,' Aron stammered. 'You don't know what you're doing.'

'Oh yes I do,' she retorted. 'We've been planning this for months. We're taking your plane hostage. The Black Aura is going to land in a private airfield and from there we'll invite the world's media. We'll expose you bastards for what you are. Happy fucking Christmas!'

'You don't understand.' Aron took a step forward. 'Look at the time. If we don't begin to drop our cargo now it'll be too late. They'll-'

'Don't move another inch!' Yvonne drew an imaginary line with the gun up and down his body, to ensure her weapon had his full attention. 'I'm going to tie you up, you son-of-a-bitch. You can keep your real co-pilot company.'

Yvonne glanced at the semi-naked prisoner lying on the floor, nodding to her as she spoke.

Taking the opportunity of her eye line momentarily broken from his, Aron launched himself towards her, grabbing her wrists, and sending the two of them careering into the cockpit. They crashed against the control panel, knocking the wind from Yvonne's lungs. She dropped the revolver, but a knee to Aron's crotch sent her attacker reeling. She threw a punch, connecting with his cheek and splitting his lip. The Captain staggered backwards. He reached out wildly to grab her but Yvonne dodged his clumsy attack, stepping to the side and pushing him off balance. As he fell, his fingertips caught hold of her jacket and pulled her with him. The pair collapsed into the captain's chair and in their struggle, rolled onto the controls. Knocking the joystick, the plane dived, at first forward towards the ground, but as the struggle intensified the controls were pulled in the other direction, causing the plane to bank upwards; sharply ascending.

The brawling pair didn't notice the plane break through the clouds. It was only when the aircraft shook did Aron and Yvonne break free from their tussle; Aron immediately leaping onto the controls and wrestling with the joystick to bring the plane level again.

Wiping the sweat and blood from his cheek he turned to Yvonne who had stood still, motionless except for a visible trembling throughout her frame. Her face was flushed of colour and her wide eyes looked past him, through the cockpit windshield, and out into the night sky.

Aron followed her gaze, tracing her line of sight to the view that had provoked so much fear.

'What. Is. That?' Yvonne struggled to speak as she fought to rationalise what she was seeing.

Dark shapes moved over the tops of the clouds. More appeared, hovering in the air. The silhouettes looked human in shape, except their heads were longer, seemingly stretched at the back and pulled into points like the tip of a comical elf hat. Their ears were equally elongated, and a drooping hunch made their backs bulge with strange, asymmetrical lumps.

'The geeks at Aura Ops have a proper name for them,' Aron explained as he took in the view. 'I can't even pronounce that Latin bullshit. I call them Satanic Cloud Elves, or Santas for short.'

'This is Santa Claus?' Yvonne felt stupid speaking such words. 'It's all real?'

'Well, sort of. Every legend has some basis in fact, right? You see their heads, like hats? Those weird growths on their backs that look like sacks? You can see how the legend was born. This, however, is the reality.'

'But… but…' Yvonne was unable to form a sentence as a million questions meshed in her mind, crossing and twisting until her thoughts were nothing more than unintelligible babble.

'Every Christmas these creatures appear,' Aron explained. 'And every year on Christmas Eve we replace the normal juice in the spray tanks for a special kind of poison. I don't know what's in it, and it doesn't hurt us, but it's like acid to these fuckers.'

One of the dark forms glided through the air with the grace of a soaring eagle and landed on the wing of the Black Aura. The plane shook as the autopilot did its best to stabilise the impact from the uninvited hitchhiker, only regaining equilibrium when Aron, once again, took control. Yvonne ran from the cockpit into the plane, stopping at the closest window and catching sight of the creature's veiny-blue skin. Its thin wrists strained with bulging sinews as it gripped onto the metal plating of the wing. Turning its head towards the window, the creature smiled, displaying a maw full of sharp, dagger-like teeth. Its eyes glowed a deep green that narrowed as they caught sight of Yvonne, dumbstruck at the window. Crawling forward, its feet proved as dexterous and strong as its hands, as it made its way towards the fuselage.

Aron swung the plane left and right, trying to shake the monster, but it held on tightly and continued its journey unabated.

'How…' Yvonne shouted to the Captain, but again her mind and mouth failed to work in conjunction, both freezing up as the first syllable was uttered.

'If we don't release that spray tonight, they'll swoop down and invade our homes, just like the legend says,' Aron called back. 'We've got to get that bastard off the wing before it does any serious damage.'

Yvonne looked back outside to see the glowing, green eyes only inches from hers. She yelped in fright and watched as it crawled down the body of the aircraft. The door on the side of the plane started to creak as the thing Aron called a Santa, pushed against it. Running towards the entrance to stop the creature from ripping it off its hinges, Yvonne was shocked to see a pair of blue hands, impossibly thin, slide through the seal around the edge of the door. Slamming her shoulder into the door, she was dismayed to find it did nothing to stop the slithering limbs from penetrating the plane. The creature's hands expanded once inside, becoming thicker and strong once again. They grasped wildly in the air, searching for, and eventually finding, the cold steel of the door handle. Yvonne pulled at the long, skinny digits, but was unable to loosen its grip, and slowly the door opened.

The crisp December air hit her hard, stealing the breath from her lungs. The monster pushed the door wider and began to crawl in.

Yvonne slammed the door back into the creature. Its body took the full force, but despite a sickening crunch, it stayed in the doorway, grabbing hold of the woman to keep itself upright.

'Aron,' Yvonne called out as she tussled with the monster, trying to push it out of the aircraft. 'Help me!'

The Captain came through from the cockpit brandishing Yvonne's revolver. A shot fired out causing sparks to fly above their heads as the bullet ricocheted off the steel work.

'Careful,' she called back to her would-be saviour.

Another shot echoed through the fuselage and

Yvonne screamed in pain, dropping to her knees as she felt a wave of agony ascend from her calf muscle.

'Don't shoot me, you idiot!' she screamed as she clawed at the monster in a bid to stay upright.

Her fingernails caught its back. The bulging membrane was soft, like rubber.

Realising the gun had no more bullets, Aron threw it to the floor and ran at the pair. Turning his side as he reached the sparring duo, he launched forward, barging his shoulder into Yvonne's back and knocking both her and the creature from the plane.

She fell from the fuselage, saved only by the speed of her reactions. One hand caught the edge of the doorway and she clung, desperately, onto the side of the plane. Her other hand was still gripped onto the back of the creature. Its rubbery skin tore against her sharp fingernails, ripping a hole down the length of its side. She watched as the skin fell open and flapped in the wind, spilling its contents into the air: a toy train, some building blocks, a jigsaw, a teddy bear.

The creature fell from sight, its dark, shadowy form nothing more than a hazy black blob as it stopped its rapid descent and gracefully soared into the murk of the night sky.

Yvonne looked up and tried to pull herself back into the plane, confused at what she'd just witnessed. Aron stood above her, watching her struggle.

'It didn't want to hurt you. It was looking for children. It's what they do. They want to give the kids toys,' he shouted at her through the wind. 'If we let them, they'd crawl into everyone's homes and give them gifts. For free!'

Yvonne's arms grew tired, lacking any strength to haul herself up. She struggled, but all she could do was hold on.

'The Government, businesses, neither would stand for that, you know,' Aron continued to shout. 'It's not the way it works. The economy would collapse.'

'Help me,' Yvonne muttered as she looked pleadingly into his eyes.

Aron smiled at her, but his eyes remained chillingly cold. Raising his boot, he stamped on her hands and watched as she fell from the plane, disappearing into the dark.

Racing to the controls, Aron pulled the joystick back, sending the plane higher into the air. Flicking another switch, a high-pitched hiss came from both sides. He smiled as he watched the air fill with his top secret cargo.

Chemicals flooded the atmosphere and rained down on the creatures in the sky. He heard them scream as huge pustules appeared on their skin. Writhing in the clouds, they zigged-zagged back and forth, but were unable to escape the poison that sent white-hot agony through every part of their beings. Aron chuckled at the gut churning sight as the growing sores exploded and their bodies began to liquefy; the spray from the Black Aura dissolving them before his eyes, melting their unsightly heads, their elongated ears and misshapen backs, whilst destroying the toys that were held within them.

Leaning back in his chair and placing his feet on the dashboard, Aron checked his flight path and put his headset on.

'Control, this is Black Aura,' he spoke into the

microphone. 'We had a bit of trouble earlier so look out for a lump of meat somewhere near Manchester. The body will need clearing away. I'll explain when I return. Besides that we're back on track.'

Removing his headset again, he spun around and stood up, humming the tune to Winter Wonderland as he walked towards the woman still sprawled on the floor and bound in rope. He knelt beside her and removed the tape from her mouth.

'Thank you, Aron,' she smiled as tears of happiness rolled down her cheeks. 'My name's Julie. I'm your co-pilot.'

'Pleased to meet you, Julie. Apologies for the rough start to your flight.' He winked.

'That bitch jumped me from behind. Before I knew anything I woke up, tied up in the cleaning cupboard. How can I ever thank you?'

'I'm sure I can think of a way,' the Captain smirked. 'Let's get you out of these ropes. I'm sure there's a spare BA uniform in the locker.' His grin widened. 'And listen, when we're done here tonight, why don't you join me for a champagne breakfast and a Christmas dip in my hot tub.'

'How could I refuse?' She blushed. 'Thank you again for saving me.'

'Well, it was nearly a disaster,' he admitted as he untied her binds, trying to ignore the smell of the frying flesh from the creatures outside. 'But everything's fine. I've saved Christmas.'

Fragmented

White. White. Red. Red.

Green. Sparkle. Yellow. Red.

Check the bulbs. Plug them in before you put them on.

Wrap the tinsel. Red. Red. Sparkle.

Level the baubles. Space them out. That's perfect. Laughter. Giggles. The fire crackles. Fresh logs. A treat every Christmas Eve. A link back to youth. A glass of mulled wine. Not for you, Jaime. Nor you, Heather. The fairy. Out the box. On a stool. Mother helps steady. Heather can just reach.

A fairy on top the tree. An angel overlooking us. A queen for twelve nights.

She'll watch over you. Keep you safe.

Warm. Relaxed. Soft. Sofa.

John sits back. Red wine. Swirls. Sips.

Savours. Swallows.

Black.

Dark.

Power cut.

Silence.

Screams. Cries. Afraid of the dark.

Calms.

Candles.

Reassures. Everything is okay.

Snowfall. Just like old times.

Cosy.

Bang.

Bang. A noise. Bang.

What is that?

Carrie gets up. Don't leave us, Mum!

Probably birds. One a month. Trapped in the conservatory. How do they get there?

Watch her go. Cuddles into Dad.

Silence.

A noise.

Scream splits the darkness. Echoes. Blood curdling.

Tears. Heather. Jaime. Cry for their mum.

They already know.

Footsteps in the hall.

Squelching.

Blood.

John scoops them up. Hush little darlings, hush. Runs to the door. The darkness opens. A face. A fist. Pow. Knocked to the ground.

Screams. Shrieks.

Jaime.

Jaime!

Thud. Tear. Crack. Splash.

Hack.

Hack.

Hack.

Splash.

Crack.

Tear.

Hack.

Splash.

Dead.

Jaime?

Heather runs. Upstairs. No. Not that way!

Have to follow.

Have to protect.

John pursues.

Footsteps. Following. Slow. Deliberate.

Creak.

He's coming.

Hide together.

Come here my darling. In the cupboard. Sshhhh...

Stay still, Heather. Hold your breath. No noise.

Closer. Closer.

Stalking.

Through the crack. Through the door. There is no face. A mask. Father Christmas. Rubber is dirty. Old. Perished.

Dirty, old Father Christmas.

White beard stained red.

White. White. Red. Red.

Hasn't seen us. Walking past. Heading into the bedroom.

Go Heather, go! Run! Down the stairs! Out the house!

John follows.

Heavy footsteps behind. Gaining.

Must protect his daughter. Blow to the back of the head. Stumble. Fall.

Black.

A fleeting moment.

Awake. Must save Heather! Back to his feet. Down the stairs.

Too late!

He already has her.

Knife through flesh. Throat split open like a pink pea pod.

Blood spurts high into the air. Daughter still twitching in killer's grip.

Fear. Anger. John attacks the killer. Pulls at the mask.

Underneath. Something vile.

Unsightly.

A mirror.

His face.

John's face.

John's face looking back.

Looks down. In John's hand, a knife dripping blood.

Hears laughter. His boss as he was fired last week. Hears screams. His boss as he plunged a knife into him. Hears the demands from his kids. Their expectations. A Christmas he can no longer deliver.

Hears the sound of his wife, Carrie, drunkenly shouting at him. Quietly whispering on the phone. Texting. Spending too long talking to others.

That smell.

Another man.

Another man!

Losing his grip. Life sliding away.

Take back control.

Taking back control!

His family now erased.

His *life* now erased.

Everything gone.

The burden lifted. Feeling free.

Steps outside.

The bitter cold. Refreshing.

Children laughing. Next door. And the house over. And the next.

Their laughter will eventually turn to screams. Screams from ungrateful brats. John can speed up the process. Calm them quicker. Saving the pain. Months of pain. Maybe years.

He smiles as he walks towards his neighbours' house. He has work to do.

Blood drips from his knife onto the snow, colouring his footprints as he goes.

White. White. Red. Red.

Behold All The Angels

The black ink of night was already beginning to taint the sky, its influence feeling unnaturally premature to the weary travellers that made their way along the winding, rural road. Biting winds blew through their grey robes and stung skin, already chapped by the plummeting temperatures. Their hands grew white in the cold as they gripped their elaborately carved staffs, and the hoods covering their heads were more a gesture than effective protection against the elements. It had been a long journey, one that was far from over.

Taal glanced back at his three companions and smiled to see the decorative patterns of gold and blue on their otherwise grey cloaks sparkle in the fading light. It was a sign, he mused. A subtle signal, reminding him that hope is a valuable asset. Even during the darkest of days it only takes one candle to light the way.

The sky above was clear and the guiding stars twinkled softly, suspended in a void of tranquillity. Cold it might be, but this winter had given them the fortune of being dry.

He regarded his companions once more as he gave contemplative thanks for their commitment. The hulking figure of Sanay with his muscular, near seven foot, frame, was made for this kind of endurance, but Kal and Maja were less physical in their prowess.

However they had made no complaint. The Sacred Whisper had chosen each member of the group, and it was from their temple in the Far East they had begun their quest; a holy pact of fellowship sealed. Now, somewhere in Europe, their journey showed no signs of ending.

The country road they followed meandered beside a series of darkening fields. It had been many miles since they had been dropped off by the last kindly truck driver willing to grant passage for a group of strange looking hitchhikers, and the stillness in the air suggested it would be sometime before another vehicle broke the isolation of this rural vista.

Stopping for a moment as the road came to the crest of a hill, Taal surveyed the landscape. As night drew in and shadows unfurled from their hiding places, the diminutive figure caught sight of something in the distance; his vision not dulled by his age.

There was no question that Taal was old, exactly how old was an answer shrouded in mystery. But despite his short stature, his wiry looking limbs and his missing teeth, Taal was formidable and extraordinarily capable. None of his companions had bested him in a sparring match, but over and above his combat skills, it was his wisdom and mastery of the Whisper – the sacred force that had all claimed them – that held him in such high esteem by his companions.

He focused, wrinkling his forehead and adding further creases to his leathery, brown skin.

On the brow of the next hill he made out a glowing rectangle: a window. An aromatic wisp of smoke caught his nostrils. The stars pulsated with a subtle shimmer in the now near-black canopy. Taal smiled.

For tonight at least, their journey could end.

*   *   *

Cold hands knocked on the door of the Inn. By the time they'd reached their destination even Taal had felt the painful bite of bitter cold on his hardy, weather-worn skin. His breath formed a misty vapour that shone in the light from the cosy interior as the door creaked open.

A large man, with thick shoulders and belly to match, stood in the doorway. His black, bushy beard had a length suggesting many years of growth, but its wiry wisps and knotted bulk showed those years had been spent indifferent to the state of his facial hair.

'Yes?' he asked eyeing the four travellers with suspicion.

'We are looking for food and a warm place for the night.' Sanay's words were stilted as he tried to wrestle with the words of a language not familiar to him.

The man stood still for a moment running his fingers through the knots in his beard.

'There's no room,' he finally uttered, his tone devoid of empathy as his eyes scanned the road and fields behind them.

'We've been travelling all day, and we have nowhere else to try,' Sanay almost pleaded, if the brute of a man knew how. Humility was a trait he was still trying to understand.

'Nowhere else for miles around,' the man explained. 'This here's an Inn, but we've no room. What's with the clothes?' he asked nodding to their attire. 'You the four wise men?'

'Three wise men, and one wise woman,' Maja answered as she pulled back her hood, revealing a pleasant, youthful face that helped to soften the Inn-Keeper's expression. 'But women always get written out of history, don't they?' She winked. 'We have been travelling for a long time and are looking for a place to stay,' Maja asked with a dialect that was flawless to the man's native tongue, 'Can you help us?'

He watched as Maja's long, black hair fell to her shoulders; her locks braided with a weave of sparkling golden thread. His eyes narrowed. His expression stoic.

'We have no room,' he repeated. 'I've only just this evening rented out my last one.'

'Do you have anything to eat?' Maja's smile remained unaltered despite the frosty reception. 'Could we, perhaps, shelter from the cold for a short while? The warmth from your fire is very enticing and our bellies are empty.'

Releasing an audible sigh of contemplation, he moved wary eyes across the band of four. Stepping forward, he leaned his head out of the doorway and searched the fields and hedgerows behind them.

'Just you four?' he asked.

'Just us.' Maja's grin grew.

'Anyone follow you? Any *thing*?'

'Not that we saw,' Maja replied.

'Have you seen anything strange? There's been a number of murders. Cattle pulled apart. You know anything about that?'

'We are merely travelling through,' she offered as testimony of innocence.

'It's dark outside,' he sounded pensive. 'You can come in. Rest up in the bar for a while. I'll fix you some food if you like.' He scratched his beard thoughtfully for a moment. 'There's more to the dark than shadows.'

The Inn-keeper pushed the door wider and stood to one side, allowing Taal, Sanay, Kal and Maja to enter.

The warmth of the roaring fire was a welcome relief; the pleasing orange glow competing with an old fashioned oil lamp that gently burnt, fixed on the wall. Tables and chairs filled the floor, three of which were occupied by people sat on their own who quietly supped on their drinks as they watched the new-comers with curious eyes.

'Drinks?' the Inn-keeper asked as he allowed himself a faint smile of hospitality.

'Yes please,' Maja responded. 'Four vodkas.'

'An excellent cho...oi-'

He stumbled on his words, eventually silenced by shock as he watched Kal remove his hood. The fire's illumination caught Kal's dark skin, revealing the raised, jagged curves of thick, grotesque scar tissue. A hideous criss-cross of wounds, not dulled even by time, encircled and scored his face, making him look both at once monstrous and tragic.

'It's okay,' Kal's voice was instantly soothing, possessing an eloquent lilt that eased their host's heart back down from a thunderous canter. 'We are preachers of peace.'

'Do not be alarmed by Kal's appearance,' Maja reassured him, gently taking hold of the man's arm and lightly squeezing it. 'Our pasts mean nothing. We can only offer our now.' She smiled, recounting Taal's words. 'And now, to you, we bring peace and money; in return for food of course.'

She winked.

'Of course,' the Inn-keeper puffed out his chest in a bid to regain his composure, embarrassed at his visible disgust for her colleague's disfigurement. 'There is little left in the kitchen, but I can throw something together for you, as long as you're not fussy. Don't mind my dog either. Size of a small horse, but heart as big as her head. Not that I've seen her for a good few hours, bloody thing.'

'Thank you for you kindness,' Maja chuckled before turning back to her companions and joining them at the free table they'd occupied.

*   *   *

'Thank you, Maja.' Taal glanced at her with approving eyes. 'As we move through this country it must remind you of your calling.'

'The calling of the Whisper is not something I will ever forget. I thought I was going mad,' she chuckled.

The others smiled empathically. They had all thought themselves pushed beyond sanity when the Whisper found them. When it invaded their minds and filled their senses. Only by accepting it, by listening to the incessant but soft voice, were they able to follow a path that took them overseas and across borders. Not knowing where they were headed, they had to truly trust their instinct to find the temple that would become their salvation; their home.

Of course if they hadn't done so, if they had resisted

the Whisper, it would have ultimately resulted in exactly what they feared: *madness*. The times of our ages are littered with such unfortunate souls.

Taal had witnessed all their arrivals over the years; having a hand in each of their rebirths as they became Servants of the Sacred Whisper.

'Whilst our past lives are behind us,' Taal spoke to Maja, but it was a lesson to all; everyday was, 'we must be open to the teachings it still has yet to tell. No story is ever truly over.'

Kal rubbed the lattice of scars across his cheek as he nodded in approval.

'My old homeland can be an unforgiving place in winter,' Maja remarked. 'But it's through such hardship that friendships are forged. The people are built of great character, and even better cooks.'

'A feast awaits us then?' Kal asked, teasingly.

'Even leftovers will be divine. There is no better land for cooking.'

Taal laughed. She still held an air of pride for her Eastern European roots. Setting foot on home soil had undoubtedly awoken this in her, but he knew this familiarity would also highlight her differences. She would discover just how much she had changed.

This journey – their mission – had more in store for them than their end goal.

'You see the world with different eyes now, Maja,' Taal gently warned. 'Guard yourself of what may come, with the resolve and reasoning of experience.'

'When I was a lad, every year I used to go to my parents' home for Christmas,' Kal offered. 'And every year I was reminded how further I had outgrown my place of upbringing.'

It was the first time Kal had talked of his past since joining the Servitude. Such conversation was normally discouraged, but away from the temple, from their training, Taal allowed this kind of self-exploration. It was another lesson. A journey within a journey.

Maja giggled. 'I can't imagine you as a boy,' she remarked to Kal. 'Nor you, Taal.'

'I never was,' came the old sage's response. A mischievous expression enveloped his face and illuminated his eyes with child-like glee, leaving his companions unsure as to whether he was joking.

They returned his smile with an inquisitive and respectful awe for their diminutive leader. Certainly with his sleight frame, reduced height and hairless head, he looked like he could have been pushed from his mother's womb in the same state as he sat before them.

'Do you remember your mother?' Maja asked dreamily.

Taal looked her in the eyes and for a moment the young woman feared she'd overstepped the mark, but a relaxing of his facial muscles showed he was not annoyed.

'When the Whisper wants me to, I remember things that have not happened yet,' he responded, lightly scratching his head. 'And sometimes, at the will of the Whisper, I can hear voices from beyond now. They float on the wind like bird song in dawn chorus.'

'You speak to your mother?' Maja leaned forward, interested in this revelation.

'Surely that's obvious, isn't it?'

Maja looked at him blankly.

'Why do you think I always keep my room clean?'

The group erupted into laughter.

'Sanay, you're very quiet,' Maja remarked as the laughter died down.

The Germanic behemoth turned to face his companions with an expression tense from worry.

'Someone's keeping a secret. A terrible secret,' he spoke quietly.

'It's not me,' Maja offered.

'No, not us,' Sanay stiffly replied. 'There's a darkness here.'

Kal and Maja scanned the room. The three people that were there as they entered still remained. They sat on separate tables and each looked entranced by their own drink.

The fire shrank back, elongating the shadows that playfully danced across their faces.

'You felt it too,' Taal acknowledged.

'What does it matter?' Kal asked. 'Are they of a concern to us?'

'When I say dark, I mean cold. Evil. Other worldly,' Sanay answered, his voice getting lower. 'I fear we may be in danger.'

'Always thinking with your head ready for battle,' Taal counselled. 'The Whisper feels muted. Suppressed. Whatever is here is powerful; ancient.'

They looked across the bar once more.

A man in the corner looked up, studying them from beneath his hat, before lowering his head again, allowing the brim of his black fedora to conceal his eyes once more. A woman sat closest to the fire, the heat of the flames unable to dry her tear-sodden cheeks. She quietly grieved, with an inaudible sadness, and did nothing to stem the drops of water that softly rolled down the contours of her face. Her eyes were transfixed on the flickering flames that fretted around the glowing remains of a log. Across the other side of the room sat an old man in a tired looking suit. Its grey wool had seen better days as threads hung from its stained lapels. The bandage on his forehead looked like it had been recently applied.

'Who is it?' Maja whispered.

The room was silent, the only noises being the crackle of the fire and the ticking of a clock as its pendulum swung rhythmically, a few feet above the mantelpiece.

'The man with the hat,' Sanay spoke without taking his eyes off his subject. 'Look at his hand, near the wrist. You see that scar? Recognise it?'

'That's no scar.' Kal replied as he studied the knotted red flesh that rose up from the stranger's skin.

'Exactly.'

'I'm sorry, I'm lost,' Maja admitted.

'It's the mark of Haverford,' Sanay answered

'Rowland Haverford,' Kal continued, recognising Maja's unchanged puzzlement, 'was a mage that terrorised Western Europe. Eventually beaten back by local shamans after he tried to take North Africa, Haverford went into hiding until his death. His house and disciples, however, still remain. A shadowy organisation, steeped in old gods and terrible rituals. They mark themselves with a design; *that design*.'

'The tendrils of the source,' Sanay added.

'Four hot stews,' the Inn-keeper announced as he

burst from the kitchen with both arms full of steaming bowls.

The Servants of the Scared Whisper returned his grin and thanked him for the food as he set a full bowl in front of each person, carefully placing a spoon to the right-hand side.

Heading back to the bar he returned with four small glasses of vodka.

'Apologies for the delay. I was trying to call my dog in. What brings you this way?' the Inn-keeper asked as he finished serving their meal.

'We are on a pilgrimage,' Maja answered. 'A holy power guides us.'

The Inn-keeper smiled an almost sympathetic smile. 'What a perfect time of year to be undertaking such a task.'

His remark was met with puzzled faces.

'You don't know? How long have you been travelling? It's Christmas Eve. Tomorrow morning is Christmas day.' His beard rose by the influence of a widening grin. 'What better time to undertake a quest of faith than on the most holy of days? I hope your travelling is both speedy and trouble-free.'

'Excuse me, sir, do you know who the man in the hat is, over there?' Sanay's Polish lacked the finesse of a native, but allowing the influence of the now muted Whisper to guide him, his voice still found enough of the correct syllables to be understood.

'Beats me,' replied the Inn-keeper. 'People come and go, and I leave them to their own business. Especially this time of year. Many a lost soul at Christmas. Sometimes this place feels like a flicker of light in the darkness. A port to call home and ride out the storm of loneliness. That's why I don't put any decorations up; not in the public bit at least. It's sad it has to be that way. But sometimes that's just the way it is.'

Bidding them a happy meal, the Inn-keeper wandered back to the bar to pour himself a drink.

'A toast,' Maja said holding up her glass. 'To our journey, and its fruitful conclusion.' Her companions chinked their glasses with each other. 'This is real vodka,' Maja continued, her glass still in the air. 'Chilled perfectly, but it will warm you through.'

They all took a sip, admiring the taste of Poland's most famous export, before tucking into the meal before them. The stew was as divine as Maja had suggested; the meat tender and the flavours rich. Silently they ate as they allowed their bodies the respite and nourishment they desired. Sanay, however, remained stiff in his seat, his eyes watching the man in the hat.

'You got a problem there, son?' The man lifted his black fedora and called out, tired of being eyeballed by the man-mountain.

'Maybe,' Sanay responded with fight in his voice.

Taal placed a calming arm on his companion but it did nothing to dampen the smouldering aggression.

'You've been looking at me for some time, with that stupid face of yours,' the man in black continued. 'You want something from me? Why don't you just step up and say it?'

Suddenly, Maja held her head and wailed in agony, falling from her chair as a wave of pain coursed through her, obliterating her equilibrium. She looked up to her companions with a confused and terrified expression as blood began to pour from her nose.

'Is that your doing?' Sanay slammed his fist on the table as he accused the man in corner.

The man smiled back. 'Seems your lady friend can't handle her drink.'

Sanay rose to his feet, his head scraping the ceiling, and stepped towards the man in black.

'I've taken down bigger assholes in my time,' the man in black threatened, unintimidated by his opponent's size. 'You want to make something of it? Be my fucking guest.'

Sanay cracked his knuckles, causing the man in the corner to stand up, his leather jacket creaking as he moved his arms into a fighting stance.

The pair squared off.

'Take your best fucking shot,' the man challenged.

Clocking what was happening the Inn-keeper ran towards the pair to break it up. Arriving just too late he caught the glancing blow of Sanay's enormous fist and was sent flying towards the wall. The man in black used the distraction and countered with a blow to the neck, followed by one to the mouth, causing Sanay to stumble backwards. Kal stood up to help his friend, but was waved back by his hulkish companion.

His opponent was nimble on his feet and darted to his side, picking up a chair and smashing it over Sanay's back. The force knocked him to the ground, but he used the position to his advantage. Reaching out, he took the man in black's ankle and pulled him to the floor. Getting back to his feet, Sanay picked his enemy up by the scruff of his shirt and threw him across the room. He sailed through the air and landed on the table where the elderly man was positioned. Collapsing the table under his heavy landing, he knocked into the old man which pushed him from his seat.

Sanay ran towards his prone opponent and grabbed his neck, lifting him up to eye level.

'Leave her be,' he shouted, pointing to Maja, who was curled into a ball and being comforted by Taal.

The defiant man smiled and spat a mouthful of blood in his face. Kicking out, he drove his knee, hard, into Sanay's groin, connecting with a sharp, powerful blow.

Sanay winced, but stood his ground, throwing his opponent once more and sending him crashing into a wall; knocking the lamp from its fitting. As it hit the floor the glass smashed and the light extinguished. For a moment the room fell into near darkness, and in that moment a scream rung out. It took a while for everyone's eyes to adjust to the faint flicker from the open fire but as they did so, the image of the crying woman's body lay broken and twisted on the ground. Two huge gashes had split her open, up her chest and across her face, blood oozing onto the floor and pooling around her corpse.

As Sanay dragged his unconscious opponent from the floor, Kal broke the silence.

'Looks like he's not the only one from the house of Haverford,' he said towering over the elderly man who sat amongst the wreck of the splintered table.

The bandage on his forehead had come free, and hidden underneath was a now familiar mark of knotted flesh: the tendril of the source.

*   *   *

Taal sat cross-legged on the floor in front of the fire, his eyes fixed somewhere through the flames and his fingers held in an intricate shape. Behind him, Maja lay, sweating on the ground, her headaches and fever intensifying. Kal knelt beside her, mopping her forehead with a towel in a vain attempt to ease her distress. Sanay paced back and forth between his two captives: the elderly man and the man in the black fedora. They both gave him their full attention as they sat, motionless, each bound to a chair by a length of rope.

'Any luck, Taal?' Sanay asked.

His mentor's silence suggested not.

The Inn-keeper sat by the bar, keeping watch and nursing his jaw. 'So who did it?' he asked. 'Are you saying it's one of these two?'

'They both have the mark of Haverford House,' Sanay replied. 'What do you have to say for yourselves?' he asked, turning his attention to the two captives. 'Which one of you killed that poor woman? Who has placed a hex on Maja?'

'We haven't done shit,' the man in black replied.

'You bear the mark of Haverford!' Sanay scoffed back.

Maja called out, unable to suppress her reaction as a lightning bolt of pain shot through her.

'The evil is growing stronger, more aggressive,' Kal commented as he held her closer to his chest. 'It always does when it's threatened.'

'You will talk!' Sanay bellowed as he leaned in towards the elderly man.

'You leave Misty alone,' the man in the hat remarked

83

with a casual swagger, at odds with the predicament he was in. 'Oh it's Haverford alright. Misty here is a wealthy aristocrat. Got inducted into Haverford some years back. Brainwashed more like. I was hired to go find him and bring him back to his family. Safely. Since pulling him from that place he seems to have gone into shock. But he's harmless. Can't stand to be close to him though, the wretch stinks something awful.'

'And what is your name?' Sanay turned to face him. 'How is it you also bear the mark?'

'Most people call me Mr. Cash, after the singer. That's as close as I like people to get.' He smiled and nodded his head in a sign of greeting. 'As for the scar? With Haverford, the only way to get someone out, is to get yourself in. Took me a year of careful planning and buttering up the right people.'

'You expect us to believe that?' Sanay scoffed.

'I'm not expecting you to believe anything.'

Mr. Cash pulled at his ropes as he tried to reposition his hands to a more comfortable angle. The chair creaked as he fidgeted with his binds.

'She's fading,' Kal announced, trembling at the thought of Maja slipping from them.

'Taal...' Sanay looked across to him desperately.

'The evil is so strong,' Taal spoke softly as sweat dripped from his brow. 'But the Whisper is breaking through. The source. It comes from there.' Without turning to look, he held his arm out and pointed in a direction behind him.

The shadow of his arm snaked across the floor, undulating against the flickering illumination. Its outstretched digit guided their eyes towards a chair. Sat on top of that chair was the man in the black fedora: the man known as Mr. Cash.

'Are you sure?' Sanay asked.

'Oh yes,' Taal replied. 'The Whisper grows louder. Stronger. I'm very sure.'

Maja screamed again as she flailed in Kal's embrace.

'Enough!' Sanay demanded. 'Demon, release her.'

'I don't know what you're talking abo-' Mr. Cash was silenced as Taal began to rise to his feet, his voice booming with ancient syllables teeming with the power of a knowledge long since hidden from the world at large.

Suddenly Mr. Cash began to shake, uncontrollably convulsing. His expression twisted as he shuffled in his seat. Sweat poured down his face as he looked at his captors and kicked his legs out wildly.

'Let me out of here!' he called, thrashing against his restraints.

'Release the girl from your spell,' demanded Sanay.

'I'm not fooling around here,' he shrieked, his voice growing higher as he tried to undo the ropes around his wrists. 'What the fuck is going on?'

The chair beneath him began to bow; its legs bending and warping. The wood stretched like an inflating balloon as the backrest grew, rising up until it towered above him. Two large points, white like tusks, emerged from the seat, growing out from the space between his thighs.

'Guys!' Mr. Cash shouted, as he looked to the people stood around him with shocked faces. 'Get me out of here!'

More tusks grew on the seat, surrounding the

screaming man, forming rows of teeth. A fleshy tendril slivered from a swelling on the pulsating backrest and had Taal not rushed to his aid and untied Mr. Cash from the seat, the slimy tongue would have wrapped itself around him and pulled its prey into a razor-lined mouth!

The chair roared as it bent and twisted; its wooden limbs growing and flailing like the tentacles of an octopus.

Mr. Cash rolled to safety as the chair charged on its four legs toward Kal and Maja. Sanay blocked its path, and the chair reared up, launching itself at him. The pair tussled, but the strength of the creature was too much. Pinning him down with its thrashing appendages, it opened the huge jaw in its seat, preparing to bite into his face. Defending his friend, Kal struck the monster with his staff and knocked it back, but a swipe from one of its slippery tendrils sent him crashing to the floor.

Again the creature charged; its prey the prone body of Maja. She tried to move, but the fever had taken hold, weakening her. Defenceless she watched the creature run towards her, its teeth growing longer as they anticipated sinking into the soft flesh of their victim.

A fist struck the monster and halted its course. Another fist and another. Mr. Cash followed his initial attack by diving onto the strange beast. Rolling on the floor with it, he refused to let go as it hissed and gurgled. The pair fell towards the fire as Mr. Cash kept up his attack. The wooden surface of the monster's body slid over his. Its teeth gnashed and gored, biting through the man's leather jacket and tearing off chunks of flesh. Blood flew high into the air, but the man was relentless in combat.

As the pair rolled into the fireplace they quickly set alight, the screams of the man drowned out by the demonic babble of the monster.

The flames grew in intensity, blinding them all for a moment, before the writhing mass of the sparring pair eventually fell still.

'My God!' the Inn-keeper exclaimed as he came out of his hiding place. 'A changeling!'

'A real nasty one too,' Sanay remarked, wiping his wounds.

Maja walked towards the fire with a sorrowful face.

'I'm sorry, Mr. Cash,' she spoke softly to the burning remains. 'Thank you.'

As she turned to walk away, a flaming tendril launched from the fire and wrapped around her leg, pulling her to the floor. Using her as an anchor, the burning figure of the changeling, more gelatinous lump than chair, heaved itself back into the room. Squealing with a demented anger, it threw its tentacles about the room, warding off any potential attackers.

Calmly, Taal stood his ground and breathlessly whispered a word of ancient origin. The ropes fell away from the wrists of the old man Mr. Cash had called Misty. His features remained expressionless as he passively surveyed the scene in front of him.

'It's me you're after!' he called to the creature that stood, burning in the room. 'It's this!'

Pulling up his shirt, Misty revealed a growth just below his nipple. The area rose in two small bumps, and within those bumps two reptilian eyes peered out. Scales surrounded the area, gradually fading into Misty's skin, but not before the emergence of a set of nostrils, and a half-formed mouth.

'I've been incubating this thing for years.' He let a tear slip down his cheeks. 'They call it The Master. Some say it's Satan, the Devil himself! I'm nothing more than a piece of meat to them! A host for this thing!'

He ran towards the changeling, and fought past the tangle of tentacles, gripping hold of the monster.

'You dare not hurt me!' he laughed as he reached into its gapping maw and pulled out its slobbering tongue. A dark, green liquid sprayed Misty as it gushed from the stump of the severed wound. Dragging it back into the fire, Misty shouted to the shocked onlookers. 'Get petrol, oil, anything flammable. Fire is the only way to be sure!'

He laughed as he wrestled with the demon; a monster unable to hurt his precious cargo, even if it meant harm to itself. The Inn-keeper raced towards them with a Jerrycan of petrol and threw it at the freakish pair.

A fireball erupted, knocking the Inn-keeper on his back and causing the others to shield their eyes. They watched the flames flare into a carnival of greens and blues. Misty kept his grip on the changeling until at last the monster and the man were nothing more than blackened husks of charred meat.

The room fell into silence for a moment, the crackling of the fire the only thing to puncture the respectful quiet.

'A changeling?' Maja turned to Taal.

'Loathsome creatures with little intelligence. They are powerful but they can only follow orders,' Taal explained. 'And even then they have a penchant for being easily distracted. It seems it had quite the taste for human females.'

'And what was that thing on poor Misty's chest?' she asked.

'I cannot say for sure,' Taal admitted. 'Perhaps it truly was the Devil. It was certainly powerful enough to evade detection from the Whisper.'

Maja wiped blood from her nose and rubbed the sweat off her forehead. 'If it's gone why am I still feeling so unwell?'

'My apologies,' the Inn-keeper cut in. 'I wasn't aware you'd be so sensitive to my protection spell.'

With a wave of his hand and a silent word he smiled and watched Maja's colour return; relief spreading across her face.

'There's much more elegant protection magic,' Maja smiled back. 'What do you need it for?'

'Call me oversensitive,' he replied, 'but when trouble started brewing I acted quickly. Today I encountered something so ancient, so pure, I was driven to help the best way I could.'

'What do you mean?'

The Inn-keeper held his finger to his lips in a gesture to keep quiet and motioned them to follow him. Leaving the Inn via the backdoor, they saw a barn a few metres away with lights glowing from the inside. A large dog came running out and greeted its owner with a wagging tail and an affectionate nuzzle into his legs. The Inn-keeper stopped for a moment and greeted his beloved pet.

'There you are,' he spoke with a soft voice as he stroked the excited animal. 'Have you been a good girl? Have you been keeping a look out?'

Standing up straight again, he led them all into the barn, followed by the shaggy canine. As they entered into the hay-filled building, the Inn-keeper began to speak.

'A couple came to me earlier today in desperate need of shelter. They were seeking protection, to be hidden from the darkness that pursued them. I had no room, except for the old stable out back. The woman was heavily pregnant and, well...'

The four gasped as they saw a manger lined with a blanket. Nestled inside was the sleeping form of a peaceful, newborn baby. Above his head, lights danced in a way even Taal had never witnessed.

His two parents looked towards the travellers and beamed with an expression of love; the purity of their emotion washing through them all, enveloping their senses in an overwhelming euphoria. Without any commands from their leader, all four Servants of the Sacred Whisper instinctively knelt before the manger, mesmerised by the shimmer of radiant beauty that surrounded the child.

The sky above was clear, and the guiding stars finally rested, twinkling softly.

For tonight, at least, their journey could end.

A Touch Of Frost

'Please touch me… Like you did before.' Her attempted confidence was overshadowed by desire; a feeling of lost wonderment washing through her words. 'Please… if you're there… touch me again.'

They all sat in silence transfixed on her performance. It was Sarah that ended the quiet, unable to take the humiliation any further.

'Stop it,' she begged, throwing a napkin at Nellie and causing the others to burst into hysterical laughter.

The flowing wine had undoubtedly made the impression funnier, but Sarah's unintentional catchphrase had only been spotted when the first series of Ghost Gazers was finishing its national television debut.

Nellie winked at Sarah and shared a smile. The two had become good friends since they met on location, and their chemistry had translated well onto the screen; the pair making a fine double act that anchored the fledgling show. Nellie Starlight was the expert of the esoteric: a medium that could pick up the voices of the dead, their feelings, and at times allow them to possess her, channelling their spectral remains through the psychic's body. Sarah was the counter-balancing sceptic: the lead presenter that questioned everything, desperately searching for a rational explanation to the strange occurrences they'd witness in haunted locations across the country.

Taking another gulp of wine, Sarah washed down the last mouthful of her Duck Liver Parfait. The starter tasted good and as she relaxed back in her chair she thoughtfully took in the sight of her new friends as they indulged in the celebration of the TV crew's first Christmas meal. It was a small crew, but the better for it. Jack and Chris were their camera operators. It had been Jack's idea to create the show after a childhood obsession of the paranormal refused to fade in adulthood. Daryl was the rather nervous sound guy, a character trait that had made him a star of the show in his own right. Colin Silver was the man with the money. He owned a production company and it was his idea to take the show on after a drunken discussion at a mutual friend's wedding. Despite it being Jack's concept, Colin ruled with an iron will, shaping the brand and managing the publicity. He was prepping Sarah for bigger things. Ghost Gazers was only the beginning for this beautiful, blonde presenter.

'Love you, Sarah,' Nellie responded back with drunken sincerity as she leant over and refilled her friend's glass with white wine; her paper crown, slipping down and almost covering her eyes.

Sarah burst into laughter at the sight. Nellie looked a mess. She always played it straight on location, so it was nice to see her really cut loose. They'd struck up a close friendship, but Sarah still struggled with Nellie's supposed powers. Were they real? Did *she* think they were real? Or was Nellie a complete fraud? Laughing behind everyone's backs as she raked in a good salary for nothing more than a little play-acting.

The cameras had often picked up the presence of white glowing lights – orbs they called them – and Sarah had often felt the temperature drop inexplicably in certain rooms to freezing temperatures, but she still struggled with believing.

She couldn't, however, deny the touch.

'You ghost hussy,' Jack laughed. 'Fancy a bit of the Dark Druid, did you?'

They'd been filming at night in the ruins of Glastonbury Abbey, investigating the haunting of a spirit nicknamed the Dark Druid. Said to walk the grounds at the time of a new moon, the shadowy figure was reported to lure kids to their death. It was considered nothing but legend until one night a teenager was witnessed stepping over the edge of a crumbling staircase and falling from the height of the ruin. An investigation was carried out, but the police grew frustrated by the local children only talking of the Dark Druid. With nothing more to go on they had to lay the blame with the young girl, proclaiming she was playing carelessly in a dangerous environment.

A month later the Abbey was fenced off and locked up every night.

During the filming of Ghost Gazers' fourth episode, Sarah and Nellie had stood at the foot of the very same staircase, and it was there she felt icy fingers grip her arm and gently pull her towards the steps. The influence was fleeting but it had left a lasting impression on the presenter. One that couldn't be explained by a draft or settling foundations. This was actual physical interaction with the spirit world!

'You know there was something we didn't mention in that show,' Colin remarked, with a sly smile, exuding his familiar air of confidence, like he always knew something just a little more than everyone else. 'I discovered it after the filming, something that had been suppressed by the police.'

'Really?' asked Jack. 'What was that?'

'It wasn't the death of the teenager that forced them to lock the place up, it was something even more chilling. The disappearance of a small child.'

The gathered crew leaned closer, interested in this new macabre revelation.

'Harry Schofield was only three years old when he vanished. The local residents joined in the search, but he was never found. At the Abbey they found his trike, turned over with its wheels still spinning. Fragments of his clothes were caught on a hedge, bloodied and torn, but his body was never discovered.' Colin took a sip of wine for a dramatic pause as the rest listened intently. 'At the base of the steps they found his electronic nursery rhyme book. Cracked and damaged, its broken speaker somehow still worked and managed to splutter out a distorted song. It was stuck on loop, playing his favourite rhyme over and over: Three Blind Mice. They say, every December, on the anniversary of his death, you can hear the distorted sounds of that song playing faintly in the wind.'

'I'm calling bullshit,' Jack chipped in. 'I've never heard of that before.'

'Maybe your research isn't as meticulous as you might think,' Colin politely rebuked. 'There's more to fact finding than searching on the internet and trawling through newspaper archives. Sometimes you need to speak to people. Uncover that which is hidden. The world is full of secrets.'

'It's also full of bullshiters!' Jack tried hard not to give an accusatory glance towards his producer, but felt it happen anyway. Colin was an entertainer; that was his job. He was the one that brought the psychic in and turned the whole thing into a circus. Jack had envisioned it to be a serious research show, a quest to find out more about the paranormal. But he was told it wouldn't work. A show like that simply wouldn't sell.

The resentment had never truly left him, despite the popularity and success it had garnered under Colin's guidance.

Breaking the tension, Daryl blew into his party horn, unfurling the paper length and piercing the momentary troubled silence with a jovial rasp. Others immediately grabbed theirs and blew back in retaliation.

'So what was the scariest one we did?' he asked, moving the conversation on.

'Oh that's easy. It has to be the Ram,' Jack replied.

Sarah shuddered, 'Oh God.'

'Yes, the Ram Inn, with the mad cavalier,' Nellie joined in. 'I could feel him crawling around by the bed in the master suite. He was a terrible presence. So much malice. So much hatred.'

'He took a shine to you didn't he, Sarah?' Daryl recollected.

'He wanted you,' Nellie glanced to her co-presenter. 'You didn't know his thoughts, but I did. He wanted to wrestle you onto that bed and hurt you. He wanted to hurt you so bad.'

'Oh please,' her face began to grow pale at the thought. 'I felt horrible for days afterwards. They usually don't bother me, but that one, that night... ugh. This feeling, this threat, it got to me in that old pub and wouldn't leave. I just couldn't shake it.'

'Spirits can be known to leave their place of haunting,' Nellie grew concerned. 'It's rare, but there are documented cases of it happening. If the spirit is strong enough, if its desire is great enough, it can leave where it was once tied, and instead latch on to a person.'

'What about the old postage museum?' Colin cut in, changing the subject. 'There was some strange stuff in that one.'

'That was so fucked up!' Daryl exclaimed before necking his glass of Pinot Grigio.

'It went crazy, huh?' Colin continued with enthusiasm. 'All those orbs.'

'And the balls,' Sarah excitedly chipped in. 'All those airsoft balls in the basement. They were throwing them at us from the dark. We were literally playing catch with ghosts!'

'Now why didn't we get any of that on film?' Jack turned to his quiet friend, Chris.

Chris was not the greatest of talkers at the best of times, but as the conversation had developed he had slowly shrunk further and further into his chair, knowing exactly where this would lead.

'I didn't realise!' he protested.

'Cardinal sin of a cameraman,' Colin smiled. 'Not charging the batteries before a shoot!'

'There'll come another time,' Nellie reassured him.

'By the time I ran back to car for the spare one it had

all stopped,' Jack continued to scold his friend. 'At least we had the juice to film the twenty punches you took to the arm for being such a douchebag.'

'That bruise has only just gone down, too.' Chris rubbed his left arm as he recounted the punishment.

'That should have totally made the episode,' Daryl said through a laugh as he turned to his producer, questioningly.

'You don't want to show everything; not straight away,' Colin replied with that familiar tone of sly wisdom. 'It'll make an excellent extra for the DVD.'

'Ghost balls,' Daryl chuckled as he said it. 'Please. Please touch me!'

The group roared with laughter as he stood up and held his crotch, his face mirroring the worried frown of Sarah in the opening titles of the show.

*   *   *

Sarah stood in front of a mirror and looked over her appearance. The stillness in the toilets was a welcome respite from the crazy antics of the Ghost Gazers' Christmas party. The conversation had become more vulgar as the empty wine bottles stacked up, but the laughter had increased as a result. They were a good bunch and Sarah was happy to have landed the role as presenter for such a great team.

She smoothed her black dress against her hips and inspected her make up as she leant closer to her reflection. Her mascara had survived its brief encounter with tears earlier. Sarah had tried not to cry, but felt her eyes dampen as she'd recounted that horrible feeling she'd suffered since filming at the Ram Inn.

The Mad Cavalier, Nellie had said.

A monster of a man in life that was so vile, so evil, he wanted nothing more than to abuse. To hurt. To rape. Sarah hadn't been right since, and even though the suffocating dread had faded, talking about it again tonight had brought everything back.

She shuddered as the room grew colder.

A tear rolled down her cheek. Then another.

Stepping into a cubicle, Sarah locked the door and shook her head. Allowing the tears to fall, she silently told herself to stop, but knew this was a demand that had lost all persuasion.

For a few moments she let herself weep, but a gentle knock on the door provided enough motivation for her crying to momentarily halt.

'You okay?' It was Nellie. Her Irish accent softened with compassion.

'Yeah, I'm fine,' Sarah lied. 'I'm just being silly. Probably the alcohol.'

'Are you sure?'

'Really, I am.' Another lie.

'Okay sweetie. I know you're not, but that's your call.' Nellie didn't want to force the issue. 'If you want to talk, you know where I am. Remember, you can't lie to a psychic.'

'Thanks,' Sarah said, her head in her hands.

'Love you, beautiful,' came Nellie's comforting response.

'Love you too.'

Focusing on the sound of high-heels against the floor tiles, Sarah listened to Nellie walking away, ending with a creak of a door, a sudden rush of noise from the joviality of the restaurant, then silence. Calm.

Sarah carefully wiped the water from her cheeks and looked to the ceiling. Why couldn't she shake it? It had happened months ago. All the other investigations had been fine. But this one... why?

Above her head the lights flickered for a moment, before giving up completely and plunging her into darkness. The cubicle was pitch black and it took a few moments for her eyes to register the faint image of her own hands in front of her.

Remaining seated, Sarah strained to listen out for the restaurant staff. She expected to hear them telling the other customers that everything was going to be fine, that the power would be restored shortly. But she heard nothing. The place was silent.

Standing up to leave, Sarah decided it was best to join the rest of the group, but something made her stop. She froze, held her breath and listened again.

There was something moving, but not walking, not footsteps; this was something else. Something shuffling, dragging, crawling.

The air turned cold as a chill prickled her arms. Crouching down so she could hear better through the gap at the bottom of the door, she listened again.

The sound grew louder. More distinct.

A scrabbling on the floor. Hands on the tiles, dragging themselves closer.

Unnerved by the strange sound against the eerie quiet, Sarah sat back down and pulled her legs to her chest, putting her feet on the toilet. She curled into a tight ball, trying to keep herself hidden whilst her mind raced. What was happening? Could it be someone in trouble? The last time she heard those noises was in the dark, a few months ago at the master bedroom of a haunted public house.

The Ram Inn.

No.

The cold numbed her shoulders, turning her breath to mist.

A bang against the cubicle door made the walls shake and Sarah closed her eyes, burying her face into her knees to mute the scream she tried desperately to conceal.

The door shook again as someone pummelled it from the other side. Frozen to the spot, Sarah was trapped. Her pupils widened as adrenaline flooded her body, the floor glowed brighter as her body heightened her senses. She looked around. Could she crawl over the top of the cubicles, maybe make it to the window on the other side?

Another bang halted her escape plan before it had already begun, driving the thoughts from her mind.

Sarah's eyes fixed on the hinges as they rattled against the weakening screws.

And then it stopped.

Silence.

After a few minutes she dared to put her feet back on the floor.

Come on, you idiot, she told herself, trying to force some rational thought through her. *It's nothing. It's not the Mad Cavalier. Probably a staff member coming to check the toilets in a power cut.*

Reaching for the door she slowly turned the lock and

allowed it to gently swing ajar. Waiting for a moment she gingerly stepped forward. Could she hear something? A sound? A whispering? Her name over and over again?

Don't be an idiot, she told herself again. *You're better than this.*

Pushing the door wide, she stepped out into the darkness. The place was empty and the murk heavy. The glow of the white tiles appeared lessened out here, and quickly faded into the gloom only a few feet from her. But within those few feet she could make out a shape on the floor. An arm. A hat. Something shimmered, something white. A frilly collar.

Slowly it began to rise, standing in front of her. A smell of decay filled her nostrils. An earthy musk laced with the aroma of rot. A face glowed with an off-blue in the darkness. Its mouth opened and black blood trickled over its chin, running down its scraggly beard.

A faint and weak voice strained from the figure. 'I've followed you,' it rasped. 'I want you.'

Sarah's eyes widened as the cavalier staggered towards her, one lumbering step at a time. With nowhere to run, she slowly walked backwards, hoping to seek sanctuary in the cubicle she'd just left. But feeling the wall push into her back she realised she must have changed direction in the dark.

The exit was on the other side of the ghost.

She was cornered.

The ghost reached out a spectral hand and she felt his fingers radiate with a sub-zero chill.

'It was you,' she whispered. 'You left the Ram and followed us. You were at the Abbey, not the Druid.'

His demented eyes grew clearer as he drew closer,

emerging from the dark. They were full of evil. Full of hate.

'W-what do you... you w-want from m-m-me?' Sarah asked, cowering against the wall and barely able to talk.

He opened his mouth wider to speak. Blood poured down his chin and splashed onto the floor. His eyes flickered with rage as his outstretched fingers edged closer to her terrified face. There was no stopping the tears now.

'I want... you... to... touch me,' the apparition announced with unexpected clarity, suddenly halting his advance and standing up straight.

'What?' Sarah asked confused.

'I want you to touch me. Please touch me. Touch me again.'

The voice sounded familiar, the accent changing to a friendly Irish drawl.

'Nellie?'

'Surprise!' a chorus of voices announced as the lights came on.

Before Sarah could make sense of what was happening a large cake was thrown at her face, splattering her in a mess of cream and sauces. Wiping the cream from her eyes, Sarah could make out the smiling faces of Colin, Jack and Daryl. Chris was holding a camera pointed at her and Nellie was beaming from ear to ear, dressed in a cavalier outfit with fake blood pouring down her chin.

'Merry Christmas, sweetie,' Nellie said giving her friend a big hug and kiss on the cheek before turning to the camera. 'Merry Christmas from all of us at Ghost Gazers.'

Colin smiled as they all headed back to their seats to finish the meal. *The restaurant had been a gem helping to set up the prank*, he thought to himself. *This kind of promo is perfect for viral marketing. And besides, it'll make a great extra for the DVD.*

*   *   *

Cleaned up, full of food and merry with Christmas cheer, Sarah hugged her friends as they all said goodbye at the end of the night. The meal had been great, their glasses never empty, and as for the prank: her friends were brilliant. That cavalier costume had been a great gag. She'd best get used to these things if she was going to be a TV star.

The excitement of her future career lifted her spirits further, keeping her company on the quiet streets as she walked back home.

She was so lost in her own thoughts that she almost didn't notice the upturned trike underneath the flickering lamppost. The wheels were still spinning, and as she slowed she saw the silhouette of a small boy stood motionless, staring in her direction.

The wind began to blow, but she could just make out what he was singing.

'See how they run. See how they run.'

Behind her, she felt the presence of something else. Someone taller. Someone towering over her.

A hand grasped her shoulder, its touch colder than death.

A Demon In Santa

The following is a direct scan from my Primary School *Creative Writing* exercise book. I was 10 years old and in the last year of Primary School.

Thank you to my Mum for having the foresight to keep these books so well preserved.

Rest In Peace Mr Roberts, the teacher that marked this story and gave me enormous encouragement with my writing.

If you are unable to read my infantile handwriting, I have typed it up on the pages immediately following the scan.

A Demon in Santa

"Oh well", said Santa, "another christ christmas." "Here's your sack," said his wife, "and be quick it's turkey tonight." Little did Santa realize, that in his sack was a gremlin! "I hate christmas," thought the the gremlin, "people laughing, giving presents and not even being just a little bit naughty. But this year it's all going to change, yes it's all going to change."

As Santa landed he thought of his wife, and eating turkey by the fire. Suddenly he stopped thinking about jolly, happy thoughts, he began to think of naughty things and smashing everything! His fat, jolly red face changed to a pale colour, and his eyes changed into yellow sharp eyes! His hands turned into claws! The gremlin had gone inside Santa and was making him do nasty things. He dived in a chimney and wrecked half

The of it, on the way down CRASH!!! Went Santa as he landed in the fireplace and put out the remaining fire. "Those choclates look good," said Santa looking at the Christmas tree. "Yum," said Santa, this is too good to waste." Then he ate the whole tree! "Yuck," said Santa, "that bit taste like dirt with stingingnettles." Meanwhile upstairs Jimmy, the boy, had been woke by the bang Santa had made. "What was that?" said Jimmy, "I'd better find out." He crept down the stair and looked around. SMASH!!!/CRASH!!! Jimmy looked round and saw a plate come flying out of the kitchen. He burst into the room. But nothing was there. Jimmy picked up a torch and his longest and sharpest knife. He ran upstairs to get his clothes on when a ~~mird~~ came through his window. "Please help us," said the elf, "Santa has a gremlin inside of him. It will make him wreck ~~& the~~ Christmas! But if all the presents ~~preson~~ aren't delivered by ~~t~~ midnight Santa will disapper and the ~~wille~~ skies will be black forever!" "I'd better be goin then," said Jimmy as he rushed downstairs and put his shoes on. He ran out of the house and saw a trail of sweet wrappers leading into the house next door. "Oh no," said Jimmy, "that's Mr Killys house." Jimmy crept up to the front door, or what was left of it, and look in. There he could see Santa drinking beer. "Yuck!" I said ~~whisper~~ Jimmy, "that's horrible." Then after Santa had finished the last bottle he was drunk and would do anything for sweets. Jimmy set a trap up with a torch, string and a pile of sweets. Then Santa came walking along and spotted the sweets. He picked up one, what was tied on the string, it pulled the torches switch and turned it on. The gremlin ran out of Santa and out of sight. "Santa!" Jimmy shouted, "you've got to get all the presents in the stockings by midnight." "I'll do my street, you do the rest. Tom had the last gift. He put it in a stocking. Then, Bong, Bong, Bong. He had done it on the very last second. "Phew," said Jimmy, "that was lucky." "I thought Christmas was a goner."

Good- one of the best christmas stories I've read in a long time.

108

A Demon In Santa:

'Oh well,' said Santa, 'another Christmas.'

'Here's your sack,' said his wife, 'and be quick, it's turkey tonight.'

Little did Santa realise that in his sack was a gremlin!

'I hate Christmas,' thought the gremlin. 'People laughing, giving presents and not even being just a little bit naughty. But this year it's all going to change, yes it's all going to change.'

As Santa landed he thought of his wife and eating turkey by the fire. Suddenly he stopped thinking about jolly, happy thoughts, he began to think of naughty things and smashing everything! His fat, jolly red face changed to a pale colour, and his eyes changed into yellow sharp eyes! His hands turned into claws!

The gremlin had gone inside Santa and was making him do nasty things.

He dived in a chimney and wrecked half of it on the way down.

CRASH!! went Santa as he landed in the fireplace and put out the remaining fire.

'Those chocolates look good,' said Santa looking at the Christmas tree. 'Yum,' said Santa, 'this is too good to waste.'

Then he ate the whole tree!

'Yuck,' said Santa, 'that bit taste like dirt with stinging nettles.'

Meanwhile upstairs Jimmy, the boy, had been woken by the noise Santa had made.

'What was that?' said Jimmy, 'I'd better find out.'

He crept down the stairs and looked around.

SMASH!!!

CRASH!!!

Jimmy looked round and saw a plate come flying out of the kitchen. He burst into the room. But nothing was there. Jimmy picked up a torch and his longest and sharpest knife. He ran upstairs to get his clothes on when an elf came through his window.

'Please help us,' said the elf. 'Santa has a gremlin inside of him. It will make him wreck Christmas! But if all the presents aren't delivered by midnight Santa will disappear and the skies will be black forever!'

'I'd better be going then,' said Jimmy as he rushed downstairs and put his shoes on.

He ran out of the house and saw a trail of sweet wrappers leading into the house next door.

'Oh no,' said Jimmy, 'that's Mr Rilly's house.'

Jimmy crept up to the front door, or what was left of it, and looked in. There he could see Santa drinking beer.

'Yuck!' said Jimmy. 'That's horrible.'

Then after Santa had finished the last bottle he was drunk and would do anything for sweets. Jimmy set a trap up with a torch, string and a pile of sweets. Then Santa came walking along and spotted the sweets. He picked up one, what was tied on the string, it pulled the torches switch and turned it on.

The gremlin ran out of Santa and out of sight.

'Santa!' Jimmy shouted. 'You've got to get all the presents in the stockings by midnight.'

'I'll do my street, you do the rest.'

Tom had the last gift. He put it in a stocking.

Then Bong, Bong, Bong.

He had done it on the very last second.

'Phew,' said Jimmy, 'that was lucky. I thought Christmas was a goner.'

Dear Constance

19th December 1842

Dear Constance,

I trust you are well, dear sister, and your pregnancy continues to be uneventful. As I write I am watching the hurried dance of a turbulent blizzard, the likes of which I cannot recall; not even in the days of our youth, when the weather seemed to be frequently wilder than the tame, grey drizzle we now suffer daily, regardless of the season.

Indeed, so bad is the bluster and heavy the falling flakes, that I've offered the visiting Father Feeney a bed for the evening. No man, let alone one of holy state, should be forced to walk home across the moors in such terrible conditions.

Cousin Greta and Aunt Alice arrived safely for their Christmas break. It is nothing short of a marvel to witness just how our dearest cousin has grown. The person that stood before me in the hallway was no longer the young tom-boy with grazed knees, but a graceful and charming woman!

I wish you could be with us, but your husband is right: you shouldn't be expected to travel at such a late stage in your pregnancy, and if anything were to happen as a result of my keenness for tradition, then I should never

be able to forgive myself.
You shall be missed, but I shall continue to write.

Yours lovingly
Gabriel Milton.

21st December 1842

Dear Constance,

I cannot say when my letters will reach you, but I hope the delay will be short. The snow has not stopped falling, and we have become prisoners inside my house. I shall, however, continue to write, and when the roads and fields are clear once more I shall send them all to you. With this method put into practice it will serve two purposes: it will ensure that I remember every account, for my memory has not improved with age, and secondly it will allow me to feel that you are with us; if not in person, then at least you can be here in thought.

I hope you and George are keeping well and not suffering the same onslaught from the elements as we are forced to endure. Christmas is a time for family, and I am saddened by your absence.

But enough of my maudlin meanderings. I have played host all day, and perhaps my enforced positivity is beginning to wear.

The blizzard does not abate.

This afternoon Father Feeney attempted to cross the fields and back to town, but the drifts proved deceptive and the good Father had not traversed half of the first field when he fell from view. Aunt Alice screamed as she witnessed him disappear beneath the snowline, and despite my best efforts of rescue I was unable to find him.

Thankfully, Father Feeney was a man less delicate than I presumed, and within a few minutes I heard him call out, coupled with a waving arm that signalled attention whilst he pulled himself from the snow covered pasture.

The poor man looked blue, a mixture of shock and cold no doubt, but he quickly returned to a more healthy shade after a few moments in front of the fire and wrapped in my warmest blanket. So it would seem that Father Feeney may be an unintentional guest, but what better company to have over Christmas than a priest!

Martha and Charles will be able to cope with serving another. Cousin Greta may be full of modern values, make no mistake, but she has not forgotten her manners, and is no trouble. Aunt Alice on the other hand has not changed, and remains a boorish handful; a lady for whom, it seems, everything pales against her lofty standards of perfection.

Still, they are all less fortunate than I, and Christmas is a time for giving; for sharing prosperity. We are well stocked for the festivities that lie ahead, therefore my house is open to them all, and I shall indeed look forward to playing the perfect host, regardless of how unusual I find it to remain full of charm and good grace without my usual morning walk.

Yours lovingly
Gabriel Milton.

22nd December 1842

Dear Constance,

This morning, as I made my way downstairs, I was met by Martha who wore a puzzled expression. She greeted me good morning and led me into the drawing room where she pointed to a large box, wrapped in the most colourful of paper and tied with a bow.

My delight turned to wonderment as she explained how the present was discovered: In the early hours of the morning, Charles had opened the front door, armed with a spade and an intent to clear the snow, creating a path to the road. As he stepped out into the bracing cold, Charles found the box wrapped in the same state it was presented to me, simply sat upon our doorstep in the receding gloom of early dawn. Martha went on to say that Charles could see no presence of the anonymous gift bearer: no person, no note, not even a set of footprints.

Now of course, we both know that Martha and Charles are advanced in their years, and have a tendency to turn to superstition in order to rationalise the uncanny. Charles called it a gift from Satan and wouldn't have it in the house, but Martha stopped him before he could set alight to it. And whilst she agreed that it must have come from something supernatural, there was nothing to say its origins lay in hell. In fact dear Martha believes it to have come from a place somewhat more northerly than the fiery pits. She believes it to be a Christmas present from the angels, a gift for saving Father Feeney and offering him a place to stay.

Of course, I believe nothing of the sort. Falling snow

could easily cover footprints made in the night, erasing any trace of the path taken by our mysterious gift bearer. The question, however, of who it could possibly have come from, or how they delivered it to us through such treacherous conditions, still perplexes me.

I must confess I am intrigued but I will play the game and wait until Christmas day.

Is it from you, dear Constance? Are you and George playing a marvellous jape on your older brother?

Tricky as it may be to set up such a stunt, I would not put it past either of you to meticulously plan such a prank.

Following the discovery of the present, the day has been spent in a fine mood, with everyone lending a hand to prepare the house. Even Aunt Alice seemed to enjoy herself as we indulged in the latest fad of bringing a fir tree inside and decorating it with painted cones and gingerbread men fresh from Martha's oven.

I have never seen the house so alive, and I must confess a tear of happiness rolls down my cheek as I recall the atmosphere of the day. Dinner was a jovial affair full of wit and laughter, with Greta proving herself to be quite the accomplished joke teller.

I must also remark that Father Feeney has been very interested in you, dear sister, especially when I mentioned you being married to a man of government and living in London. I do hope you find such a revelation flattering.

I must be off to bed, but no doubt will write again soon.

Yours lovingly
Gabriel Milton.

23rd December 1842

Dear Constance,

I wonder if this snow will ever thaw? Will I ever be able to take the road into town once more and greet Mr. Mayfield in the post office? I look at the letters I have written to you, amused by the growing pile. I hope this mountain of words is a testament to the love for my sister, even when you are absent.

Today has been a strange day, and I wonder if the enforced confinement is starting to irritate my guests? Certainly, the lack of fresh air within our home seems to have resulted in a most peculiar musk about the house. Its aroma is unpleasant, yet too subtle for me to trace its origins. Also apparent was a change in mood about the place since yesterday's frivolities; most notably from Father Feeney. Dinner seemed pleasant enough until Cousin Greta began to talk of her new-fangled ideals: explaining how woman should be allowed to work for themselves; how they are masters of many skills, equal to that of any man. Whilst I took this poppycock as the zeal of youth and went to wave it off, Father Feeney roared with laughter and pounced on the debate, lecturing the poor woman before I had a chance to interject.

He retorted that women are nothing more than hosts; a vessel to nurture something of much greater power.

Greta was ready to retaliate when the good Father turned to all of us and continued his offbeat sermon. 'Real power,' he said, 'doesn't come from skill or strength; not in the modern age. Real power comes from government. From political influence and leadership.' Please bear in mind, dear sister, that these are his words I quote, not mine: 'A man can kill one person, maybe a few, but to kill hundreds, only a politician can do such a thing. Massacre his enemy whilst sending his own to slaughter, and be thanked for it. That is true power.'

Aunt Alice saw that Greta was about to argue back, and glared at her across the table, but it did no good.

'What good did war ever do us?' Greta protested.

'Chaos,' Father Feeney replied. 'There's a pleasure in destruction that cannot be compared. A release that brings us closer to our purest form. The world swings in a balance, and during winter it threatens to fall into the shadows. Take Christmas for instance. Christmas is the darkest time of year. A time of pagan magic and ritual. This is not a time for God, this is a time for Pan. Or The Devil. Whatever you wish to call him.'

Of course I paraphrase the conversation, but I hope to have captured the essence.

One thing I am certain of is the shocked faces from all us. The priest just smiled at our bewilderment and tucked into his dinner, noisily slurping and belching as the rest of us stared at him in silence.

I weakly laughed and desperately tried to move the conversation on, but the damage was irreparable. Our meals were finished in the most stilted of atmosphere, and we all said our pleasantries, retiring early to bed, except for Father Feeney, who I can hear merrily laughing in the drawing room below me.

My mind still turns with his unexpected sentiment; even writing it down has not exposed a deeper meaning as I had hoped. Perhaps the meditation of sleep will present his true message.

To add even more to my woes, the strange smell has worsened throughout the evening. I hope my guests do not think ill of me, although I'm sure the priest's outbursts have commanded the attention of Aunt Alice and Cousin Greta over the minor quibble of an aromatic irritant. I would search for its source, but the events of the evening have exhausted me. Tomorrow I'm sure Charles and Martha will aid in cleansing the house and restoring the festive atmosphere that we so relished in yesterday.

For now I must rest my weary mind and hope for much needed tranquillity in my slumber.

Yours lovingly
Gabriel Milton.

24th December 1842

Dear Constance,

Why did I do it? Why didn't I leave it all alone? God, I don't even know why I am writing to you. It seems absurd. I can barely see in the dim light of the attic, but this is where I am hidden. My body shakes with cold and fear, making my handwriting erratic, but I am terrified that I will drift off to sleep if I do not do something to keep myself awake. I cannot say for sure how many hours I have been here, concealed; listening out for

Oh Constance. How do I explain?

This morning I woke from a troubled sleep to find the stench had grown stronger and more repugnant. Heading downstairs, Martha greeted me with a troubled look. She explained that Father Feeney had not slept, and had spent the whole night drinking through my bottles of port and whisky. I could hear his strange laughter from the drawing room. He was muttering to himself in between his bouts of mirth; cursing with a shockingly blasphemous tongue.

A chilling fear crept over me as I went to confront the priest. His self-observed rant penetrated the closed door between us and his seemingly unnatural register quickly quelled the fiery agitation his improperness had invoked within me.

I shrunk back, not wanting to admit my cowardice and instead went to find the source of the rotting aroma. Martha and I followed the stench, finding it growing stronger, the closer we came to the Christmas tree. Underneath the decorated fir lay the strange present that had so mysteriously appeared on my doorstep. Pulling it out into the middle of the room, I was left with no uncertainty that this was the source of the vile stench.

Removing the wrapping paper, I lifted the lid of the wooden box, and was shocked by what I saw.

Inside the box, to my horror and confusion, was the decapitated head of Father Feeney!

Impossible, I thought, as his laughing and cursing was still emanated from the room next door; becoming even more wild and frantic as I felt my heart pound against my chest.

I tried to raise the alarm, to call the others from their slumber, but I was stricken with fear. I heard the door to the drawing room open and the laughter grow louder. Slowly, footsteps made their way towards me, echoing in the hallway.

It was the face of Father Feeney that entered the room, only his eyes held the hue of something sinister. A dark, dark red glimmered from his stare as it found me. I felt myself wilt from his gaze; such evil causing me to cower. When I saw the bleeding head of Charles in his hand, I gasped, roaring that he was indeed a monster. I tried to fight him, but his strength took me by surprise and he swatted me to the ground with ease.

I did my best to stop him but I didn't stand a chance. Beaten as I was, I found myself terrified to the point of catatonia!

Constance, my dear sister, he did such terrible things. He pulled them from their beds and dragged them down the stairs. He attacked and tore them to pieces. All of them! He laughed as he did it; dangling pieces of my friends and family in front of me. Forcing me to watch as he chewed on their entrails.

Eventually I found the strength to break free from my fugue and ran. Outside I would freeze to death, so I sprinted towards the attic where I knew I had a rifle stored.

And so I sit here not daring to sleep, recounting the things he'd said as I lay terrified beneath him; as I was transfixed on his rampage.

He told me that he broke through the walls of the spirit world; that he crawled through the earth and snow, desperate to flee the flames of hell. Attacking Father Feeney had been a chance encounter when the old man tried to cross the fields, but it had been a fortunate one.

Taking the priest's form, the demon indulged in our company, but his mission became clear. He would make a new hell, here on earth; a kingdom of his own. A kingdom of pain and suffering. He would light the darkness of winter with the explosions of gun powder, fill it with the screams of the dying. Chaos and slaughter would rule once more, and he would be king.

The house drips in blood. It runs down the walls. Martha. Charles. Aunt Alice and Greta, all pulled apart. All turned inside out. All before my very eyes!

I'm too scared to go downstairs.

I fear he has more in store for our family yet, dearest Constance. The way he talked of your husband, the power and influence of government. The ability to order men to war and bring conflict across countries. I have watched him change shape. Change appearance, to my own very likeness! Oh Constance, please don't trust anyone. Not me, not your husband. If you don't hear from me and this letter is found, please know th a   t

I

26th December 1842

Dear Constance,

I am looking forward to seeing you at New Year. The snow has lifted and my spirits are high. Forgive me for my apparent rudeness and any incoherent ramblings you may have received in my name. I have been in a fever and regrettably written many letters whilst in this stupor. I do not believe any made it to the post office, but I cannot say for certain. If you did suffer the misfortune of receiving such a correspondence from your dear brother, I apologise for the upset this fleeting lunacy may have induced.

I am confident any misgivings will not interrupt your term. In fact I am most positive you are carrying a son. I am also equally positive of his imminent arrival; certainly I feel we shall be blessed to witness his first cries together.

I do hope you like the gift I bring with me. I write with the utmost sincerity when I mention that my Christmas guests saw your present, and they found it to be an absolute scream.

Tell George I look forward to seeing him too, and that as gentlemen I would be delighted to share a private drink and conversation with him about current affairs and matters of government. I'm sure between us we can find a way to light up the darkness of winter.

Yours forever
Gabriel Milton.

The Thirteenth Day

Bleary eyes did their best to focus as Nick reached for his phone. The sprightly ringtone hammered into his head, pummelling his pulsating temples as he tried to fight a wave of nausea brought on by his sudden movements.

Mum.

He sighed at the name displayed on the screen and hit the cancel button before rolling onto his back and waiting for the sick feeling to subside.

'You're awake then?' a voice drifted up from his bedroom floor. 'Who was that?'

'My Mum,' Nick groaned rather than spoke.

Slowly shifting onto his side, he gradually focused on his friend, Gary. His friend smiled in return and lifted his head from the pile of clothes that had been his make-shift bed.

'Drink?' Gary said, holding out a glass of water. 'And neck some of these.'

Nick leant forward and took the painkillers, washing them down with a mouthful of welcome liquid refreshment.

'I feel like crap,' Nick complained as he sat upright, realising he still had his clothes on from the night before.

'Me too,' Gary grinned. 'But good party, hey?'

Panicking for a moment, and tapping his pockets, Nick calmed as he found what he was looking for.

'No one nicked my Zippo!' A sense of triumph in his discovery momentarily distracted him from his thumping head.

The Zippo lighter had been a present from Lucy this Christmas, a friend he hoped would become much more. She'd only given it to him a few days ago and Nick was paranoid that a light fingered acquaintance might take as much of a shine to it as he had.

'The inhabitants of 77 Wells Road once again raised the party stakes,' Gary proclaimed. 'Your post-Christmas bash was even better than the Christmas one, I reckon.' He was chuffed his best mate had ended up living in a house of cool kids. For the first time in their lives they got to hang with a bunch of real party animals. Bongs, booze and birds. All were part of the new scene they had found themselves in after Nick had moved into this house. At first he'd been upset that the University's halls of residence were full and that he'd have to find a shared house somewhere in the city, but that apparent misfortune had turned out to be one of the best things that had ever happened to him.

Nick and Gary had both enjoyed going back home for Christmas and seeing their parents, but after three months of independence at University and parties every week, neither of them could wait to leave their childhood homes once more, get back to their new life and cut loose.

Nick took another sip of water. 'What happened?'

'I can't remember much,' Gary confessed. 'Dan set up the beer pong, which was fine. I think it all got a bit messy after Tom broke out the chillum. Steve puked over Jayne and they had a blazing row.'

Nick chuckled at this memory. 'Oh fuck, yeah, that god damn chillum.'

'Then you decorated the front door after taking a hit and decided to *get some air*.'

'Oh god.' Nick felt himself go green as he remembered the feel of half-digested turkey sandwiches pouring from his mouth; the slop of mushed up bread across his lips.

'After that it gets a little hazy. The room started spinning and we were both going to whitey. Must have come up here and crashed out.' Gary stood up and opened the curtains, smiling at the crisp glow of a clear January morning. 'It's a bit chilly in here, mate,' he said as he rubbed his arms in a symbolic gesture.

'Yeah,' Nick empathised. 'Sorry about that. Night storage heaters are the absolute worst; you can never set them right. The landlord's such a tightwad he won't replace them. I've tried to complain, but who are we? Just a bunch of scummy students. Although I did blag a gas heater from my mum when I went back home.'

'And you're not using it?'

'We were, but people kept losing the backdoor key, and without the lock you need to wedge it shut. As you can imagine, the act of putting something heavy in front of the door to keep it closed is quite beyond the guys here, so it just kept blowing open. The wind came right through the house and knocked the pilot light out. The whole place ended up stinking of gas.'

'Gross.'

'And a little dangerous. So I packed it away until we

can get a better regime on backdoor security.'

Gary laughed. 'Another fine plan ruined by incompetent housemates.'

'Quite,' Nick agreed as he edged off the bed and got to his feet. 'That's the thing with these guys. You want a bag of weed by this afternoon, they're on it; but ask them to do something remotely sensible like remember bin day or keep the door shut and you're screwed. What time is it?'

'Eleven thirty,' Gary responded, after checking his watch.

'Oh man, shall we go see what the damage is?' Nick half joked with a tremble of trepidation in his voice.

'I suppose we must,' his friend mirrored his mock-fear and they both laughed.

A waft of stale alcohol and marijuana smoke flooded their nostrils as Nick opened his bedroom door to reveal a landing decorated from the excesses of a wild party.

'Fucking hell, man,' Gary laughed. 'That's some serious carnage.'

Handprints of something brown and sticky marked the walls, empty bottles and crushed cans littered the sodden carpet, and a puddle of vomit pooled beside a man, his back to them as he lay, sparked out, in a foetal position; the state of his shirt suggested he'd spent a while rolling in his own puke before finally passing out.

'Man down. Man down!' Gary whooped with glee. 'The chillum claims another scalp!'

'Steve?' Nick asked as he gently knelt beside the unconscious body, trying to rouse them.

'Oooooo, he stinks!' Gary's face screwed up as he

caught the acrid aroma of bile. 'That is not cool, man. *We* may have passed out, but fuck me, at least we weren't in that state!'

'Will you shut up for a second and help me, please?' Nick's quick glance and cutting tone scolded his friend for his lack of compassion.

Taking his friend's brow beating, Gary knelt down with an apologetic look and together they gripped Steve's shoulders, carefully turning him on his back.

'Jesus Christ!' Gary gagged, repulsed by the sight. 'What the fuck?'

Nick's face drained of colour and he instantly let go of his friend's sodden shirt. Discovering his hand was wet, he dragged his palm across the carpet, wiping blood from his fingers. His friend's skin was bone white and his clothes soaked sanguine from the dripping lacerations that criss-crossed his face and sliced through his chest.

'Steve...?' Nick softly spoke, gripping his friend's shoulder and gently shaking him. 'Steve...?'

A gurgling sound in Steve's throat signified his rousing consciousness, even if it was weak. As he came round, his eyes slowly opened, taking a moment to focus on the concerned young men that knelt before him.

'Steve!' Gary called out, as he leaned closer; the initial shock subsiding. 'Who did this?'

'In... here... The... house...' Steve's reply was faint and laboured.

'In the house? Someone's in the house?' Nick repeated. He went to quiz him further, to ask him the hundred questions that bubbled in his mind, but as he watched Steve's head roll back and his eyes close, he knew they would never open again.

Nick felt his own body go numb. Pins and needles buzzed about his skin as a silent tear rolled down his cheek. He felt the gaze of a horde of invisible faces. Scanning the landing, there was no one there, but every door threatened to burst open. Every bedroom held the possibility of a killer; a maniac hiding in the dark waiting to finish the slaughter.

Turning back to his best friend, he saw Gary dialling a number on his mobile. Panicking, Nick launched at him, knocking Gary's phone from his hand.

'What did you do that for?' Gary protested, as he picked his phone up from the blood-drenched floor.

'Ssssshhhhhh,' Nick hushed. 'We've got to stay quiet. Whoever did that could still be here.'

'But-'

'No buts. We've got to get out of this house. No noises, no fuss.' Nick was surprised by the sudden clarity in his thoughts. 'We get out, then we call the cops, the ambulance, the fucking whoever. Okay?'

He held his friend's hands and pulled them to his chest.

'You with me?' he asked.

Gary nodded, his body shaking as the peril of the situation set it in.

'Okay, let's go.'

Gary set off first, slowly. The urge to run was driven by the adrenaline pumping through his veins, but he held back from his flight instinct and carefully tiptoed, one quiet step at a time. He had to be measured. Controlled. With each step he scanned the scene in front of him, looking out for a hidden threat.

The handprints on the wall were dried blood, Gary could see that now. Arterial sprays had peppered the magnolia paint job, dripped down the banister and drenched the floor. Something awful had happened last night while they been under the blissful influence of a marijuana-induced slumber. In the clutches of dreamless sleep a nightmare had unfolded around them. His stomach churned as he placed his foot onto the next step and watched as his weight forced blood to rise from the carpet.

Nick followed behind, his eyes trained on the space they'd just left. The four doors on the landing remained motionless but any one of them could swing open at a moment's notice. He dared them to do so. To break the tension that dried his throat and made him grind his teeth.

Reaching the bottom of the stairs, the hallway was even worse. Blood had splattered the corridor, dripping down the walls as it dried into brown streaks and collected on a floor littered with torn clothing and broken glass. Across the hallway they could see the front door; their escape from this hellhole.

Seeing their goal a few metres away, Nick bolted towards the door, but was stopped by Gary pulling on his arm. Confused, Nick went to push him off, but when his gaze was directed to the lounge his words of disagreement changed to a whispered, 'Holy shit.'

Hard to make out in her hiding place, but unmistakable with the streak of purple hair in her fringe, they saw Lucy cowering under a table and hidden behind sofa cushions. Her eyes were wide and fixed on the two of them.

'You okay?' Gary whispered, trying his hardest to project his voice while at the same time keeping it at a low volume.

Lucy didn't respond but continued to tremble, huddled under the table.

Slowly, Nick and Gary crept into the living room. The place was a mess. Broken bottles and crushed cans. Overturned ashtrays and furniture tipped on their sides. The blood was so thick that it hadn't dried and slowly slid down the floral wallpaper like treacle. It was an awful scene, but it was also empty of threat.

'You okay?' Gary asked, his voice rising as his confidence grew.

Spurred on by his own heroic awareness, he didn't wait for an answer and rushed towards her, holding out his hand in an offer to pull her up.

Lucy shook her head, refusing to move from her place under the table.

'Get away!' she whispered, her eyes widening. 'You've got to get away. Hide!'

'Come with us,' Gary begged. 'We're going to get out of here and get hel-' He stopped abruptly as something stroked his shoulder.

Instinctively, Nick leapt back noticing something move out of the corner of his eye and latch on to Gary.

'Fucking hell! That scared the crap out of me!' Nick laughed with relief as he realised what it was.

A Christmas decoration had fallen from the ceiling and softly landed on his friend.

'Fucking hell!' Gary sounded annoyed.

They both laughed, but quickly Gary's smile ceased, becoming an expression of pain.

'Shit, that kills,' he said trying to brush the decoration from him.

'A piece of foil? Don't be such a pussy.'

'I'm serious. That really fucking-'

Gary fell to his knees as his face screwed up from agony. Nick went to help his friend, but Lucy caught his hand, pulling him under the table. Pushing her back, he reached towards Gary, but as he caught sight of the foil streamer wrap around his mate and tighten against his skin, he stopped, frozen with shock. The decoration pulled against Gary's flesh like cheese wire, slicing into him. Wounds opened up across his shoulder as the foil cut deep into his skin and sawed through his muscle.

Another streamer dropped from the ceiling and landed across his face, slicing into his cheek. A third drifted down and wrapped itself around his chest. Nick shook off his shocked-induced trance and reached out to his friend. Gary thrashed wildly in agony. Seeing his mate's helping hand, he reached out and their fingertips met. Taking hold, and pulling him closer, Nick didn't see the streamer crawl up Gary's arm until it had reached his own wrist. Its touch was sharp, and felt like a wasp's sting. Instinctively Nick pulled away, cradling his hand and allowing Lucy to pull him back under the table and behind the sofa cushions.

Gary screamed as more streamers landed on his body and wrapped themselves around him. He went to pull them away, clawing at the decorations that circled his throat, but their sharp edges cut into his digits, severing the flesh and slicing the bone so they dangled uselessly from his palm; hanging on by the loosest of tendons.

Blood poured down his neck as the foil's metallic bite

took his nose from his face and uncovered his cheek bone. Small pieces of his own meat fell to the floor: a fragment of ear, a scrape of skin, a chunk of chin and tongue. All splashing into a growing puddle of blood.

His struggle weakened as he lost strength, collapsing to the floor with his arms outstretched for help. Greens, reds and gold slivered about his body, tightening their attack and dicing him into smaller and smaller pieces until his body was nothing more than a putrid puddle of human mince.

'What the fuck is happening?' Nick turned to Lucy.

'I don't know,' she admitted, trying her hardest to fight back tears. 'The whole place just went crazy. People starting screaming and running around. At first we thought it was a joke, but then we saw...'

'What?' Nick asked, trying to make sense of it. 'What did you see?'

'That!' she pointed to the slop that was once their friend. The foil streamers were crawling in the crimson butchery like earthworms in dirt. They appeared at home in the slaughter. 'The decorations started attacking us. The God damn Christmas decorations! I've been here all night. Too scared to move. Oh Nick!' Lucy wrapped her arms around him.

The pair embraced for a moment, and Nick absorbed the warm feeling of her body against his. He'd longed to hold her since the first day they met, and her touch brought him renewed courage.

A movement on his thigh caused him to jump, but the muffled ringtone in his pocket made him realise what it was. He fished the phone from his trousers and cancelled the call.

'Not now, Mum,' he mouthed as he shook his head.

'Nick,' Lucy shrieked as she struck his arm.

Turning, he saw her intended target and pulled at the piece of tinsel that had looped around his bicep. Shaking it free before it got a good grip, the pair looked about them. Glittery strands sparkled in the light as pieces of tinsel crawled towards them like snakes. Their hiding place had been rumbled!

Taking each other's hand, they emerged from under the table and ran towards the hallway. A crimson bauble hurtled through the air, launched from somewhere unseen. It exploded into razor sharp shards that flew in their direction. Ducking, they narrowly missed the deadly shrapnel as it embedded itself into the wall behind them.

Another bauble tried its luck with the same attack, but Lucy and Nick made it into the hallway before the missiles found their target. Slamming the door behind them, they felt the impact as the glittery shards hit the other side of their makeshift barricade.

'Are you okay?' Lucy asked, noticing the blood trickling down Nick's arm.

'I'm fine,' he reassured her. 'It just grazed me. Let's go.'

Grabbing her hand again, the pair ran through the hallway and towards the front door. The sunlight shone through the frosted glass looking like sweet rays of freedom. Their escape was so close.

Suddenly a dark shape rose up, blocking the light and their exit. The conical, needle-coated tree undulated in front of them, its branches shaking and reaching out towards Nick and Lucy. The monstrous tree was almost as tall as the ceiling and filled the width of the hallway. Blood dripped from its spiny limbs as it somehow lumbered forwards with the heavy plod of an animal four times its size. Roaring with the ferocity of a lion, it continued its building charge, causing Lucy and Nick to stop in their tracks.

Without a word spoken between them they turned and headed back, deeper into the house. Seeking shelter they dived into the nearest doorway. Lucy immediately yelped as she felt something bite her ankle. Looking down she saw a miniature snowman gleefully chewing on her flesh. Kicking it in the face, she watched the figurine fly through the air and hit the wall, exploding into shards of cheap china. A movement from the corner of her vision made Lucy direct her gaze to the window ledge. A nativity scene had come to life, the model figures of Mary, Joseph and the three wise men, fixed their glowing red eyes on her and smiled, fang-filled grins, whilst a bawling Baby Jesus demanded meat as he burbled on the blood of his last victim.

'Fuck that shit,' Lucy mouthed with horror.

'Lucy, come on,' Nick shouted, grabbing her hand and pulling her into the next room.

He slammed the door shut, and with the help of his friend, pushed a bed in front of it, upping it on its end and leaning it against the only way in or out.

'This is Paul's room,' Nick offered, clocking Lucy's wonderment about their surroundings. 'We'll be safe here. The grumpy miser couldn't give a rat's ass about Christmas so it should be free of anything festive.'

Taking a moment to catch his breath, Nick walked across the room and picked up a chair stood next to a desk. He held it above his head and launched it at the window. The glass reverberated, but held strong; the chair bouncing off and crashing next to Lucy's feet.

'Double glazing,' muttered Nick, disheartened.

'We're on the ground floor,' Lucy offered. 'Can't we just open it and climb out?'

'Two problems with that. One: there's a basement flat patio below. And two: Paul used to flick cigarette butts out the window. The downstairs neighbour complained and the landlord sealed the window shut. Never mind, we'll just... shit!'

'What's up?'

'My phone. I must have dropped it in the lounge. Have you got yours?'

'Have I fuck!' Lucy scoffed. 'The place was like a riot scene last night. I have no idea where any of my stuff is!'

Nick kicked the wall in anger.

'Hey calm down. We're safe for now.' Lucy placed her hands on his body and slid her arms round his waist for a hug.

'Lucy, what the hell is going on?' he asked as he reciprocated her movements and entered into a comforting embrace.

'I don't know,' she answered. 'The only thing I can think of is Damo. He got drunk, and you know what he's like, started going on about this book he got for Christmas. Started drawing chalk circles on the kitchen floor and chanting some stupid incantation. Crazy bastard might actually have summoned something.'

Nick shook his head in disbelief and looked over her shoulder. The street outside was quiet; the sun shone with an enticing beauty but the cold temperature had kept people indoors. These short winter days meant that it wouldn't be long before darkness fell. They needed to get help.

Releasing Lucy, Nick made his way to the desk in the corner of the room and wrote *Help Us* on a piece of paper pulled from a lifeless printer.

'What are you doing?' Lucy asked.

'I think we're in luck,' he beamed as he held the homemade sign against the window.

Looking down the street, Lucy's expression grew to match his. A few metres away and getting closer was the unmistakeable high-vis jacket of a police officer.

As she walked by the house, the trapped duo beat against the window and waved, attracting the attention of Police Constable Vikki Warwick. At first she looked puzzled at the pair, but through hand signals and an attempt to show her their bleeding wounds, the constable appeared at least curious enough to investigate.

Lucy and Nick jumped for joy, unable to suppress a cheer when they watched PC Warwick head to the front door. They heard the sound of the doorbell ring. Then a firm knock. Unable to answer it, they struggled with the bed jammed against the door. Trying to break down their homemade barricade, they listened carefully as they did so, hoping the front door was still unlocked. As they heard her try the handle, and the door slowly swing open, they were thankful it was.

'Hello?' PC Vikki Warwick called out as she gingerly opened the door.

The hallway was dark and the house smelt of

something awful. Exactly what she could smell, Vikki was struggling to identify. Cigarettes. Weed. Day old alcohol. Teenage sweat. And something else…

Stepping into the house she feet her feet squelch on the carpet.

Gross, she thought as her touched something sticky on the wall.

A Christmas tree filled the width of the hall in front of her, blocking her path.

What the hell? she thought. *It's got to be students. Are they playing a prank on me?*

From another room she heard a mobile phone ring.

'Hello?' she called out again, still receiving no response.

Putting her back against the wall, she began to edge round the tree that blocked her path. As she brushed past its branches she felt the needles. They were sharp. Unusually so. Wincing as she felt one draw blood from her hand, she paused for a moment to take in the ridiculousness of the situation.

What am I doing? she asked herself. *I'm basically hugging a Christmas tree. This is stupid. These kids are fine, they've probably got a camera on me. I don't have time for pranks.*

Heading back round the tree to leave, she felt a branch move across her body, pushing her against the wall. Confused by the sensation she stopped for a moment trying to work out what it was. Finding nothing hidden amongst the branches she went to carry on round when a spikey limb thrust forward catching her leg. Its sharp edges easily tore through the fabric of her trousers and ripped into her skin, puncturing her left thigh. She howled in pain and instinctively clutched her gushing wound, feeling her leg grow wet with her own blood. Another branch shot forward, knocking her hands away from her injury and slicing through her right wrist. Rotating needles spun, deep into her arm, drilling through her flesh and out the other side; embedding itself into the wall behind her. Trying to fight back the pain, Vikki reached to activate her panic button with her free hand, but another branch caught her, driving through her palm and forcing the arm above her head; trapping her where she stood.

PC Warwick's blood dripped down her face as the branches rotated inside her wounds, twisting and pulling at her injuries. Pain seared through her mind, stealing her screams. She struggled, trying to fight the tree, but it leant forward and bellowed a terrifying, impossible roar.

Tinsel began to wrap around her ankles, constricting so tightly she felt something snap. Jagged ends of bone broke through her flesh as, wide eyed, she watched two branches emerge from the thicket of greenery. Aimed towards her eyes, the Police Constable was powerless to stop their approach as they crept closer and closer; at first brushing her eyelashes, then closer still, pushing into the conjunctiva membrane. As the force increased, the needles began to do their damage, ripping into the corneas like white-hot needles.

PC Warwick screamed as the branches filled her eye sockets, pushing her mangled eyeballs back into her skull. Blood gushed down her cheeks. Her wails cracked and faltered as the agony become unbearable. Another branch shot out, filling her mouth and muffling her cries. She shook her head, trying to wrestle the gag away, but to no avail. As the needles began to spin inside her mouth they tore her teeth from her gums, making her gag on the blood that filled her throat. She screamed harder, trying to fight through the muffling effect, but another branch lashed out and speared the soft flesh of her neck, ripping open her windpipe and silencing the shrieks of the broken officer. Her muscles went limp as she lost consciousness; her lifeless corpse still pinned to the wall.

Nick and Lucy continued to pull at the bed, eventually moving it from the door. They'd heard the police officer enter, and were desperate to warn her. They knew she wouldn't believe them, that she had to see it for herself; only then would she get help. But they hadn't expected her to be so brazen as to walk straight in and head past the Christmas tree. They had to stop her.

By the time they'd dismantled their make-shift barricade and stormed out into the hallway, egged on by the rush of a possible escape, PC Warwick was already a pin cushion of pine needles, dripping claret coloured blood onto a squirming pile of tinsel.

Nick and Lucy stared at the corpse in horror.

Something shot past their heads, whistling as it went through the air. Lodging into the wall, they saw it was a red Christmas candle.

'There's no way past!' Nick shouted, seemingly giving up all hope.

'What about the backdoor?' Lucy offered as she pulled his arm, leading him back into the house. 'It's our only hope! If we can get there we'll jump the wall and once safe we'll call the cops.'

Hoping that his housemates had been true to form,

and not been as organised as to have sorted a new backdoor key from the landlord, Nick headed to the back of the house, making a quick detour to dive into the lounge and pick up his dropped phone.

The handset was vibrating when he got to it. Cancelling his Mum's call he ran back into the hallway, only to find Lucy caught in what looked a spider's web. The weave spread the width of the corridor, and as Nick tried to free his friend from the entanglement, he realised the plastic strands weren't cobwebs at all, but wires. The fairy lights all came on at once, illuminating the unnatural web and making the bulbs instantly too hot to touch. His hands stung from the heat as they brushed against the lights in a frantic bid to untie her. Behind them they heard the lumbering shuffle of the Christmas tree as it grew tired of the Police Officer's corpse and made its way towards its new victims. Lucy screamed, but when Nick glanced up, he noticed her gaze was fixed elsewhere; her shriek of terror was not for the demonic, carnivorous conifer, but for another reason entirely. Above her something half crawled, half scuttled down the web-like lattice of fairy lights; something   vile.
The evil smile of the approaching threat broke the angelic ideal with which its face was originally sculpted. Wings grew ragged from its back and fangs protruded from its open mouth.

As the seven inch Christmas Fairy scuttled down its trap, all Lucy could do was watch.

Finally unknotting the tangle of wires, Nick freed his friend; and not a moment too soon!

Jumping away from the web, they missed the fangs of

the creature by centimetres, but they had no time to celebrate their escape. Taking each other by the hand they ran to the backdoor. Nick stumbled and collapsed as a bolt of pain shot up his leg. Clutching his thigh, he found a Christmas candle buried deep into his flesh. A streamer crawled towards him, catching his foot. Shaking it free, he turned to something even worse rolling towards him.

Snapping a mouth of holly teeth like a crazed, demonic pac-man, a wreath charged towards him. Lucy grabbed his hand and hoisted him to his feet. He groaned in anguish, but did everything he could to keep upright.

'Come on,' she shouted, 'we're almost there.'

Turning to run, the wreath proved quicker and landed on his back. Biting deep into his side, the monstrous decoration tore a huge chunk of flesh from his torso. Collapsing to his knees, Nick searched into his pockets and pulled out his Zippo. Striking the flint, he pushed the flame towards his attacker and watched as it quickly ignited, retreating from its attack.

Not stopping to see the thing become a ball of blue flame, Nick got back to his feet, aided by Lucy, and they dashed towards the back door. A bauble exploded. Then another. Shrapnel caught them, but they refused to succumb to their injuries. Their lungs burnt and their muscles ached, but they kept running. Their escape was so close.

As they reached the back door, Nick stopped for a moment. Ducking a number of spear-like candles, he crouched below the coat rack and pulled out the discarded gas heater, the one he'd borrowed from his parents. Turning the switch on the canister, he heard the rush of gas and smelt its metallic aroma. Wheeling it towards the house he pushed it forward and watched as it careered down the hallway. Pivoting to one side and hitting the wall, it tipped onto one wheel then fell on to its side, continuing to spew gas into the air.

Lighting his Zippo once more, Nick silently thanked Lucy for his coveted gift, then threw it on the ground.

The flame didn't take long to catch; burning the stack of unopened letters, the collected pile of cardboard that never quite got to the recycling box and eventually the cheap curtains that hung in the halfway.

Running out the door and diving over the wall, Nick never got to see the moment the flames and gas met, but they both felt it. An explosion threw glass out onto the street, and they could hear the crackling of fire inside as an inferno engulfed his student digs. A strange cacophony of squeals and hissing drifted from the building, trumped and silence by a terrifying roar that could only have come from the monstrous Christmas tree.

Lucy and Nick sat behind the safety of the garden wall and smiled to each other; elated at the sounds of the demonic decorations' demise.

A sprightly ringtone erupted from Nick's pocket. Fishing his phone from his trousers, he pressed the answer button and placed it against his ear.

'Hi Mum,' he said between deep breaths.

'Hi Nick. Hi,' came a bubbly and enthusiastic voice. 'Sorry to bother you. I just wanted to call to ask, have you taken your decorations down? Only it was the sixth yesterday – the twelfth day of Christmas – and it's unlucky to leave them up any longer.'

'Don't worry Mum,' he replied, the sound of sirens drifting down the street and getting closer. 'That's already taken care of.'

The Wassailer

The decorations glistened with a tacky charm, but did little to enthuse the sterile hospital surroundings with festive cheer. The walls were clean and had recently been repainted, but the reflection of the harsh illumination from the strip lights against the magnolia brickwork was soulless. The bland lack of atmosphere was all-consuming, stifling the tinsel and foil streamers that had been crudely stuck to the polystyrene ceiling tiles.

Special Constable Aimee Forrest purposefully walked down the corridor with an armful of presents and forced a smile, whistling the melody to *Little Town of Bethlehem*.

It doesn't matter about the surroundings, Aimee thought to herself, *Christmas is what you make it.*

She tried her best to believe her own thoughts as she walked with an uneven step and an exaggerated shuffle.

The hospital brought back painful memories.

It had been a hard few months for both her and her brother. The physiotherapy was working well, but she'd been warned the limp could be permanent. Her arms and ribs had healed, but her leg had twisted as she'd stubbornly walked with a hairline fracture, determined to be back on duty as soon as possible. Whilst her commitment to the police force was admirable, her refusal to rest caused her foot to sit at a ten degree outward rotation as it healed, resulting in her steps going out of line and a pronounced limp in her walk. A reminder of four months ago. A reminder of *that* day.

She shuddered.

Aimee was thankful she was back on duty. If nothing else the events of the summer had taught her she was a fighter through and through. The police force was her calling, and she was committed to it. She hadn't hesitated in signing up for tonight's shift. Hardly anyone wanted to work Christmas Eve, but she had been more than willing, happy to take up the slack whilst her full time colleagues had a chance to be at home with their families.

Her family had been ripped apart by the events at the Oracle building site and the aftermath that followed. Like a slow rot, it had crept through the entire family, weakening their minds and isolating them at a time when they needed each other the most.

Aimee saw that now, and today she'd begin to put things right.

She was due on the beat in a couple of hours, but first she had to see her brother.

Pressing a buzzer beside a door, she patiently waited for it to unlock. The nurse smiled as Aimee walked past him, eyeing the sign on the wall.

Psychiatric Ward. Please check in with reception.

She hated the fact that Jake was here.

'Miss Forrest,' she spoke politely to the receptionist who noted her name on a computer. 'I'm here to visit Jake Forrest.'

'Of course, Miss Forrest,' the receptionist eyed her over the top of his half-moon glasses. The wire frames did little to hide his tired eyes. 'Those presents,' he stared at the brightly wrapped boxes in Aimee's arms, 'do they contain any of the following?'

The receptionist placed a laminated sheet on the desk in front of the visitor. She scanned the photographs: alcohol, pens, pencils, cutlery, aerosol sprays, headphones, skipping ropes, medication, a necklace.

'New novels by his favourite authors, a few colouring books and some crayons,' Aimee declared in response. 'Crayons okay?'

'They're fine,' the man replied not even making eye contact as he took the laminated sign back. 'In you go.'

'Jake's through here,' the nurse approached her with a welcoming tone in his voice. 'Follow me, he's been so excited to see you.'

*   *   *

The sincerity of the nurse's words were called into question as Aimee sat down in an armchair opposite her brother. He gazed out the window and had barely reacted to her entrance; his vision transfixed by the outside world, the gentle dusting of snow on an empty lawn. He appeared a little rounder than she remembered, his wiry frame beginning to fill out on hospital food.

The nurse looked at Aimee sympathetically, smiled and quietly returned to the reception area.

'Jake,' Aimee called tenderly to him. 'Jake, it's Aimee, how you doing?'

He twitched his nose.

At least it was a sign.

'Jake, I bought you some presents for Christmas.'

Jake turned and looked at his sister. His eyes looked damp, his face ashen. He eyed her uniform and his lips curled into a faint ghost of a smile.

'You came back, sis.' His voice was a barely audible rasp. 'He's been waiting.'

'Would you like a drink of water?' Aimee asked, trying to ignore his ramblings. 'I can get you a glass of water.'

The Special Constable placed the gifts on the coffee table beside them and went to stand.

'Don't go,' Jake reached up and grabbed her hand, gently motioning her back to a sitting position.

'How are you, Jake?' she asked, complying with his request to remain.

'I'm okay.' His agitated expression told a different story.

Aimee reached out and softly squeezed his hand.

'I keep seeing her. I keep seeing Laura.' Jake turned back to face the window and looked across the lawn, glowing white as a light layer of snow began to settle. 'I thought after a while here the memories would fade. Or they'd be able to fix it so that I don't have to replay that horrible moment again and again. You said they'd be able to help. But they haven't. They feed me drugs but the memories still get through.'

Jake looked down and studied his sister's fingers as they caressed the back of his hand.

'I see her face just like it was all happening again. Her blood on my hands, pouring from the wound in her stomach. I see the screaming face of *my* girlfriend, only it's not. It twists. Dissolves. Fades into the dirt.'

Aimee felt the splashing of her brother's tears as they gently fell onto her palm.

'No one believes me. They won't accept that Laura was trying to kill me. That she got Kayleigh. That it was self-defence. But that wasn't Laura. It wasn't. It couldn't have been.'

Aimee pulled him in for a hug.

'I believe you, Jake. I do. But you've got to be strong again.'

Aimee had been witness to it all, but she'd warned him telling the truth to the authorities was not the way to go. If she had done the same she'd be in exactly the same place as Jake. But try as she might to tell him of the consequences, nothing could stop his out-pourings; a mixture of grief, confusion, and eventually, insanity.

He'd crumbled, mentally, and Aimee felt responsible. She hadn't done enough to protect him.

'I expect to see her now.' Jake wiped his tears and resumed his watch of the whitening lawn. 'An arm clawing up from the ground or reaching out through the walls. She could be here right now. Listening. Watching.'

'She's gone, Jake. She won't be coming back.' Trying her best to sound reassuring, Aimee couldn't help but feel her heart break a little; a trickle of the grief she'd spent all this time trying to suppress. 'It's just us now. We're alone.'

'I haven't been left alone since the day on that building site,' Jake retorted, straightening his body to brush his sister's cuddle aside. 'If it's not Laura screaming in my head then it's the new one. The Wassailer.'

'The what?' Aimee asked, concerned with her brother's new delusion.

'The Wassailer. At least that's what I think it's called. It first appeared a few weeks back. It says it's been waiting for you.'

'Jake, please,' she interjected, but Jake kept talking.

'I first noticed it stalking the grounds outside the

hospital. I don't know if it wants me too, but it doesn't leave. I catch it in the shadows, lurking just out of sight. It has six eyes on its bulbous, pink head, and two giant fangs that obscure its mouth. You've seen the big, furry fangs of a tarantula, right? Like that, only they're dark red. Really dark red. Its arms are skinny and long, ending in pincers that look like lobster claws, only they look like they're made of bone pushed through its own skin.

'It moves quickly on four legs, but I manage to see it. Sometimes it sees me watching through the window. It stops and stares straight at me, and somehow, it smiles. I can't see its mouth past those huge fangs, but somehow I see a change in those expressionless, black eyes. I can *feel* it grin.'

Aimee shuffled, uncomfortably in her seat.

Jake continued. 'Sometimes I can feel it, even when I don't see it. When I'm all tucked up in bed. It makes a sound like the bowing of a mournful cello. It's like it isn't really there, but I can hear it, underneath the wind; behind the ringing silence in my room. And there's a smell like something moist and sodden. Like a damp dog.'

Swallowing to wet her throat, Aimee smoothed back Jake's hair.

Was he talking the truth?

The events at that building site were like nothing she'd ever witnessed. Nothing could be discounted, but Jake had been pushed too far. If he couldn't tell the difference between reality and fantasy, could she?

'I watched it tear a nurse in two the other day,' he said, keeping his eyes on the outside world. 'Cut from crotch to shoulder. Just pulled apart right in front of me. I was outside, over there,' he pointed to a bench on the edge of the lawn, near the now-frozen pond. 'It gripped her with its claws and ripped her in two then writhed in the poor woman's blood. Sadie was her name, she had nice hair.' He rubbed at his eyes as if drying unfallen tears. 'No one said a thing as it worked itself up into a state of ecstasy, clawing at its own nipples and smearing its crotch in her spilled guts.

'That's when it told me what it was. The Wassailer. The bastard dream of an exiled angel. The still beating nightmare of an undiscovered child's grave. The dweller of the twelve dark deeds. It bellowed its story at me as it brought itself to climax, yelping with a monstrous satisfaction as it plunged itself deeper into the corpse of the nurse.

'Everyone else was there, and not one person batted an eyelid. No one said a thing. Do you think they're in on it?'

His sister sighed as she gripped his knee, clenching it to show she was there.

He'd completely cracked.

Inside she berated herself. She had failed him. She had not been able to protect him; to keep him safe.

As Aimee got up to leave he squeezed her hand.

'It wants you, sis. The Wassailer. You brushed by its world when we fought the Stygian. Since then it's been intrigued by your taste. You are to be its treat. A Christmas gift to itself.'

'Monsters don't celebrate Christmas,' she said, trying to bring him down from his growing fantasy.

'Aimee,' he stood up and gripped her shoulders, pushing her back onto the chair. 'You can't leave! He'll get you!'

Jake began to shout as Aimee struggled in his grip.

The watching nurse came charging in from reception and pulled him from his sister, twisting his arm and pushing him into the wall.

'I'm so sorry,' the nurse apologised as he struggled to remove a needle from his belt, 'these episodes have become less frequent. I thought he'd be okay today. Jake,' he said turning his attention to his patient. 'Jake, if you don't calm down we'll have to put you to sleep for a while.'

Jake paid no heed to the warning and lashed out, trying to reach behind and catch hold of his assailant.

Aimee watched as Jake began to go limp. The nurse pulled a needle from his skin and carefully lowered him into the chair.

'I'm so sorry, Miss Forrest. We can't take any chances. When Jake first arrived he was highly agitated and inflicted a lot of harm on himself and others. But he's made such good progress in the last month. I thought he was getting better,' the nurse explained as he put his hypodermic needle away.

'It's okay,' the Special Constable said, reassuring him. 'And thank you.' Aimee smiled, bent down and kissed her sleeping brother on the cheek. 'Get some rest and have a wonderful day tomorrow. I'll come see you again soon. I promise.'

*   *   *

The wind was bracing as Special Constable Aimee Forrest stepped outside. The flakes were falling softly, but growing heavier. The ground was already covered in a layer of untouched snow, making the shocking streak of red appear even more prominent than it would have been.

Aimee gasped as she followed the gory trail to find a figure hunched over, face down.

Running to his aid, she righted the man and checked his pulse. His eyes opened and rolled in their sockets for a moment before settling and focusing on his saviour.

His face was cracked with age and darkened with dirt. His knotted beard stunk of alcohol and his clothes reeked of sweat.

'Are you okay?' Aimee asked.

'Uggh,' he replied, wiping blood from his face.

Checking his head, Aimee located a wound; a ragged gash across the old man's temple. Aiding the man to his feet she helped him into the back of her car. The booze had taken his speech, but his motor skills were still functional. Just.

His injury was superficial, a quick wash and he'd be fine. She'd take him to the homeless shelter on her way to the station, and if they had no room, a night in a warm cell would do him the world of good.

This was the 21st Century. There should be no excuse for anyone to sleep rough. Especially at Christmas.

It was as she opened the driver's door, and the interior light illuminated the dimming surroundings, that she noticed the footprints circling the car. Strangely triangular in shape and positioned at odd angles, as if people had played a party game and danced the conga round her vehicle.

As if the person had four feet!

Her throat dried as she took a torch from her glovebox and tracked the footprints into a storage shed beside the hospital. The door was ajar and it swung gently in the breeze, thumping against the frame as it moved back and forth on its hinges.

As Aimee shone the torch across the wooden structure she hunted for signs of movement, but everything except the door seemed static. The thumps increased as the wind picked up, causing the wooden structure to rattle against the impact.

Gusts blew past the Special Constable's ears, filling them with a rush of sound. As the ocean-like roar filled her head she swore something else danced between the aural waves; a melancholic lilt.

A cello?

Just on her spectrum of hearing sat an orchestral piece of heart breaking beauty. It wasn't a melody she recognised, but it instantly captivated her.

Then made her feel afraid.

Very afraid.

A chill ran up her body as she remembered Jake's words.

They seemed less crazy now.

A smell of something unclean, something damp, assaulted her nostrils.

Aimee leant into the car and opened up the glove box once more. She gripped a cylindrical object – a memento from that awful day at the building site - and unwrapped the cloth that surrounded it. Gripping the bone-like spike, she held it close to her as she walked towards the shed, aiming its gnarled, point towards the swinging door.

Holding her breath so as not to make a sound, she trod lightly on the snow, inching her way closer. Aimee tried to peer into the black of the shed, but its darkness was impenetrable.

The smell grew stronger causing her nose to curl in

disgust whilst the song grew clearer the closer she drew.

What the fuck was in there?

Trying her hardest to stop herself from trembling, Aimee reached out with shaking digits, ready to force the door open. The wood felt soft against her numbing fingertips.

She stopped breathing and counted.

One.

Two.

Three.

'Merry Christmas everyone!'

Her police radio burst into life.

'This is Carter finishing my last shift before Christmas. Have a great one, guys n gals.'

The message startled Aimee, causing her to jump in fright.

The scare had done her good, breaking the tension and bringing her back to her senses.

What am I doing? she scoffed to herself.

Walking back to the car, she wrapped up her weapon and placed it in the glovebox, embarrassed that she'd taken it out. What was she even doing carrying it around?

Maybe she was just as crazy as her brother?

Behind her, the tramp snored gently, lost in a peaceful slumber on the back seat.

Turning the ignition, the car fired into life. She turned on the headlights and watched as they shone into the shed. A low rumble emanated from the rickety outhouse.

'This is Special Constable Forrest, I'll be reporting for duty, working so all you slackers don't have to,' she spoke into her radio. 'Hope you all have a great

Christmas.'

It could have been a fox or badger, finding somewhere warm to seek shelter from the snow.

She pulled away and smiled as she glanced at the shed in her rear view mirror.

It's Christmas, she thought. *This isn't a time for monsters.*

Original Publications

The Girl With The Reindeer Tattoo – Burger Van & Other Stories – Michael Bray Publishing

Christmas Wrath – Bah Humbug – Matt Shaw Publications

A Christmas Tradition – Fear Is Seldom Silent – mini promo book by J. R. Park

The Wassailer – Sinister Horror Company Christmas Calendar 2016 – Sinister Horror Company

DEATH DREAMS IN A WHOREHOUSE – J. R. PARK

"This is a frigging superb short story! Think Eli Roth's 'Hostel' meets Edward Lee's 'The Chosen', crossed with a Clive Barker style search for the ultimate sensual thrill. Fast-paced, tightly-written and incredibly atmospheric," wrote DLS reviews about Clandestine Delights, a story featured in this volume.

Death Dreams In A Whorehouse collects nine blood-soaked tales of terror and intrigue from the mind of J. R. Park; a mind that Scream magazine described as 'one of the darkest places in the universe'.

Containing the stories Treats, Mandrill, Connors, Clandestine Delights, Head Spin, The Svalbard Horror, Screams In The Night, The Festering Death and I Love You.

POSTAL – J. R. PARK & MATT SHAW

From Matt Shaw Publications & the Sinister Horror Company: Two of horror's most warped minds join forces in one book.

It was a bold move, an initiative by a truly inspirational leader.

The scheme was a simple one. Each month a letter would be sent to selected people; thirteen in total. Within that month the receiver of the letter was given the lawful right to kill one person. It didn't matter who it was or how they did it.
The receiver was granted the right to commit murder with no legal consequences.

The world would never be the same again.

POSTAL

MATT SHAW

J. R. PARK

"Postal" comes across almost like the bastard love child of Grand Guignol and a comedic farce; interspersed amongst the gleefully creative and graphic deaths is a healthy injection of jet black sardonic humour and sharp slices of social commentary." – George Ilet Anderson, Ginger Nut Of Horrors.

"At the end of the day there's a lot of fun to be had in here. It's fast-paced and shovels in the blood-splattered goodness like a serial killer with a pitchfork in an all girl's dormitory. Over-the-top deaths take the front seat in this tongue-in-cheek ride through a distorted vision of our modern-day world." – DLS Reviews

"An incredible book. Violent, but not gratuitously so, thought-provoking, and funny as hell. Horror legend Matt Shaw and deserves-to-be-one-too, J.R. Park, have combined their splatter genius to come up with a modern classic. What the hell are you waiting for--grab yourself a copy RIGHT NOW!" – Amazon review

TERROR BYTE – J. R. PARK

Street tough Detective Norton is a broken man.

Still grieving the murder of his girlfriend he is called to investigate the daylight slaughter of an entire office amid rumours of a mysterious and lethal computer program. As the conspiracy unfolds the technological killer has a new target.
Fighting for survival Norton must also battle his inner demons, the wrath of MI5 and a beautiful but deadly mercenary only known as Orchid.

Unseen, undetectable and unstoppable.
In the age of technology the most deadly weapon is a few lines of code.

TERROR BYTE

J.R. PARK

"Truly a horror tale for the modern digital age."
Duncan P Bradshaw, author of Class Three

"Fast paced, action-packed, intricately plotted and filled
with technological paranoia."
Duncan Ralston, author of Woom

"He manages to combine gore, sex, humour and
suspense with a gripping story line."
Love Horror Books

"J. R. Park's new novella Terror Byte could be the story
to bring horror back to technology based adventures."
UK Horror Scene

"Jesus. What the fuck is this?"
Vincent Hunt, creator of The Red Mask From Mars

163

PUNCH – J. R. PARK

It's carnival night in the seaside town of Stanswick Sands
and tonight blood will stain the beach red.
Punch and Judy man, Martin Powell, returns after ten
years with a dark secret. As his past is revealed Martin
must face the anger of the hostile townsfolk, pushing
him to the very edge of sanity.
Humiliated and stripped of everything he holds dear,
Martin embarks on a campaign of murderous revenge,
seeking to settle scores both old and new.

The police force of this once sleepy town can't react
quick enough as they watch the body count grow at the
hands of a costumed killer.
Can they do enough to halt the malicious mayhem of the
twisted Punch?

PUNCH

J. R. Park

"It's a heartbreaking tale. I'd strongly urge anyone, looking for a straight forward raw read to buy this as soon as possible."
DK Ryan, HorrorWorlds.com

"Graphical nightmares effectively place the reader in an uneasy position."
Horror Palace

"A rousing combo of parental angst and seething evil. A great spin on the post-modern serial killer."
Daniel Marc Chant, author of Mr. Robespierre

"A hard hitting story of the darker side of life in a sleepy little seaside town."
Paul Pritchard, Amazon reviewer

165

UPON WAKING – J. R. PARK

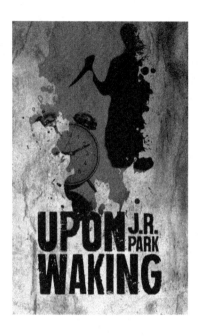

What woke you from your sleep?
Was it the light coming through the curtains? The traffic
from the street outside?

Or was it the scratching through the walls? The cries of
tormented anguish from behind locked doors? The
desperate clawing at the woodwork from a soul hell bent
on escape?

Welcome to a place where the lucky ones die quickly.

Upon waking, the nightmare truly begins.

UPON WAKING – J. R. PARK

"Upon Waking is a novel that will challenge you as a reader." – Ginger Nuts of Horror

"An absolute masterclass in gut-wrenchingly violent horror." – DLS Reviews

"J. R. Park has written one of the most painfully twisted books I have ever had the pleasure of reading. I loved it!" – 2 Book Lovers

"Justin Park needs help. I can't think of any other way of putting it. The part of his mind that this story came from must be one of the darkest places in the universe. His writing however, is just wonderful." – Confessions of a Reviewer

"It's almost like poetry in form and prose. But it's a trick. A fantastically disgusting trick." – Thomas S Flowers, author of Reinhiet

"Seriously – buy this book!" – Matt Shaw, author of Sick B*stards.

167

THE EXCHANGE – J. R. PARK

Unemployed and out of ideas, Jake and his friends
head into town for something to do.

But before long they are in over their heads.
Determined to get their friend back from the
clutches of a lethal and shadowy group, the teenagers
find themselves in possession of an object with
mysterious powers.

With their sanity crumbling amidst a warping reality,
the gang are cornered on a wasteland in the middle of
the city, caught in a bloodthirsty battle between criminal
underlords, religious sects and sadistic maniacs.

Nightmares become reality as the stakes begin to rise.
Who will have the upper hand and who will survive this
deadly encounter as they bargain for their lives in this
most deadly exchange.

THE EXCHANGE – J. R. PARK

"The most purely entertaining horror novel I've read this year. And it has unicorns!" – John McNee, author of Prince Of Nightmares

"It's gritty and tense and gets your blood pumped at the relentless in-your-face hardboiled intensity of it all." – DLS Reviews.

Amazon reviewer comments:

"The Exchange is the stuff of nightmares."

"A thrill ride of suspense, action and mystery."

"It is a real roller-coaster, packing in twists galore; plenty of gore, fascinating theologies and memorable protagonists."

MAD DOG – J. R. PARK

"You don't need my expert opinion of the esoteric to know there was something very, very wrong with him." - Father Matthews, Prison Chaplin

Mad Dog Mooney was a ghost story. A legend that spooked even the most hardened of criminals. But when he came to Darkdale prison he proved all too real.

The inmates were shell shocked by his arrival and rumours persisted of his strange behaviour, whilst accusations from the media of cannibalism were not forgotten.

As tensions grew amongst the prison population, a jail break was planned to take place under the ethereal glow of a full moon…

MAD DOG – J. R. PARK

"The final quarter is well worth the wait and is so filled with action, gore, twists and revelations that I'm almost tempted to challenge you to put the book down throughout the climax." – Jonathan Butcher, Ginger Nuts Of Horror

"It is a well-crafted story told in a unique way, with compelling characters…and there are a couple of violent scenes that had me squirming in my seat!" – Thomas Joyce, Amazon review

"If you like werewolf stories and want to read a different take on it, give this a go. Personally speaking, I'd love to see it play out on a screen… I think there is real potential here to make a truly amazing film." – Matt Shaw, author of Sick B*stards

For up to date information on the work of J. R. Park
visit:

JRPark.co.uk
Facebook.com/JRParkAuthor
Twitter @Mr_JRPark

For further information on the Sinister Horror
Company visit:

SinisterHorrorCompany.com
Facebook.com/sinisterhorrorcompany
Twitter @SinisterHC